A DOCTOR'S SECRET

LAURA SCOTT

READSCAPE PUBLISHING, LLC

Copyright © 2019 by Laura Scott

All rights reserved.

No part of this book may be reproduced in any form or by any electronic or mechanical means, including information storage and retrieval systems, without written permission from the author, except for the use of brief quotations in a book review.

❦ Created with Vellum

1

"Two minutes till landing."

Dr. Samantha Kearn took a deep breath as Reese Jarvis's calm, steady voice flowed through her headset. The Lifeline helicopter pilot could have made a living as a radio announcer playing late-night love songs. His voice reminded her of hot sultry nights, in contrast to the harsh, cold winter day she was stuck flying in.

At least she was flying.

This was it. Her first solo flight as the physician in charge. Only five more months of her residency to go and she'd graduate to a full-time attending physician. Reese landed the helicopter gently, without so much as a thud. For a moment she hesitated, her hand on the door. What if she messed up?

With a sudden burst of determination, Samantha pushed the door open and jumped to the ground. She wouldn't screw up. She was confident in her training. And maybe she was finally putting her past behind her, too.

With renewed vigor, she followed Andrew, the flight

paramedic on board, and helped him slide the gurney from the hatch in the back of the chopper.

Samantha's sweeping gaze gauged the distance from the helicopter to the building. The small community hospital didn't have a rooftop helipad; they would be forced to cross the expansive and mostly empty surface parking lot to find the hospital entrance and then finally the intensive care unit.

She'd already gotten a brief report from the ICU attending physician. Her patient was Jamie Armon, a thirty-eight-year-old woman who had originally come in with flu-like symptoms which had grown increasingly worse over the next several days. Fearing there was something more complex wrong with her, they'd requested a transfer to a larger tertiary care hospital.

Samantha impatiently tapped her foot as the elevator rambled to the third floor. Andrew noticed and offered a wan smile.

"Almost there."

She nodded. "I know." What she didn't know was how their patient was doing.

Inside the hospital's small ICU, her first glance at the monitor over the patient's bedside made her heart sink. As a rule, patients needed to be stable prior to transport, but right now, Jamie's heart rate and blood pressure teetered on the edge of a very steep canyon.

Samantha steeled her resolve. No way was she going to lose her first patient on her first solo flight.

"How much dopamine to you have her on?" She looked at the nurse as Andrew began switching all the IV connections to their smaller, compact transport models.

"Not sure, maybe around seven micrograms per kilo per minute, maybe a little more." The Cedar Ridge Hospital nurse appeared flustered as she thrust a stack of printed paperwork at Andrew.

Samantha felt a flash of pity. Smaller hospitals didn't get a lot of experience with very sick and complicated patients. From what she could tell, the nurse wasn't getting much support from the physician either. No wonder she was frazzled.

"Let me see." Samantha looked at the bag, then at the pump for the rate. She quickly did the math, verifying the patient was getting twice as much as the nurse had told her. "She's over the maximum limit, has her blood pressure always been that low?"

"Yes. No matter how high I titrate the medication, her blood pressure won't budge. The doctors here aren't even sure what's wrong with her." The nurse's bloodshot eyes were wide with anxiety.

"What are her labs?" Samantha took the paperwork from Andrew and paged through it. "She needs more volume. Double the rate of her maintenance fluids. She's low on potassium, too. Do you have a supplement we can hang before we go?"

The nurse nodded. "I'll get it."

Samantha wanted to see the radiology results, but they didn't actually print them on film anymore. When the nurse returned, Andrew took the supplement and hung it on the IV pole he'd already set up on their equipment.

"Pull up her most recent X-ray," Samantha ordered.

"I'm not sure it's been read yet." The nurse fiddled with the controls on the bedside computer until the image bloomed on the screen. "We took it ten minutes ago after placing a new central line."

The picture was grainy and not as clear as Samantha would have liked. She filed the information on the new line away and glanced at Andrew. There wasn't anything more they could do other than get this patient to Trinity Medical Center as soon as possible. "Okay, let's go."

She and Andrew packed Jamie up and quickly wheeled her out to the waiting helicopter. The wind was bitterly cold, and Samantha tugged the blanket more securely around their patient.

With Andrew's help, they loaded the patient into the chopper, then climbed in after her. As soon as they were settled with their helmets on, Reese asked, "Are you ready back there?"

"Good to go," Samantha confirmed, before placing the extra pair of headphones on Jamie's head. They were necessary in order to communicate with her, although Jamie appeared to be pretty much out of it. Even as she watched, Jamie's blood pressure dipped lower.

Reese was conversing with local air traffic control, giving coordinates for their flight plan, so she waited until he was finished.

"Reese, what's the fastest you can get us to Trinity?" As she spoke, she increased the dopamine medication, knowing it wasn't going to help much since it was maxed out. The knot in her belly tightened. If the blood pressure didn't respond, she'd have to add another vasopressor.

"We have the north wind behind us now, so we should be able to make it back to Milwaukee in forty minutes. A light snow is beginning to fall, though, so I may have to fly at a lower altitude to avoid the freezing rain. It will add time to the trip."

Normally the idea of flying in freezing rain bothered her. She'd learned in her training how ice coating the blades could down a chopper faster than a clay pigeon. But Reese's voice was so unflappably steady she didn't argue.

"Do what you can to get us safely to Trinity as soon as possible."

"Roger that." Reese lifted the chopper off the ground and gently banked to the left.

"Hey, Dr. Kearn, I'm not feeling a pulse." Andrew was holding his fingers on Jamie's carotid artery.

Samantha wanted to tell Reese to go back, but that wasn't an option. She pulled the blankets aside and noticed the skin along the entire left side of the patient's chest, the same side with the new central line, was puffy, the tissue clearly filling with air. Just then, the chopper took a hard bump. As she was unbelted and perched on the edge of the bench seat, Samantha almost fell face-first onto the patient.

"Sorry, are you all right back there?" Reese's even tone eased her alarm, calming her shaky nerves.

"Yes, but we have a problem. She's crashing. Can you hold this thing steady?"

"If I need to slow down and lower my altitude, I will," was his immediate response.

"I need to insert a chest tube; she has a tension pneumothorax." Samantha quickly dug in the flight bag for the necessary equipment. Maybe she should have waited back at the hospital, requesting a better chest X-ray before leaving the ICU with their patient.

She hoped and prayed her error didn't cost this patient her life.

"Now?" Andrew's voice rose an octave. "I've never done an in-flight chest tube."

"Watch closely, because we're doing one now." Samantha didn't let on that she'd never performed the procedure at thousands of feet in the air either.

"Okay, I'm reducing altitude," Reese informed them.

The helicopter's flight smoothed out. Samantha took a

large bore needle and catheter and quickly inserted it between the patient's fourth and fifth ribs. Jamie moaned and flinched beneath her hands. Andrew managed to connect the small portable suction machine to the end of the catheter.

"I have a pulse." Samantha couldn't prevent the wave of relief. Thank goodness the chest tube worked.

"Blood pressure is up, too." Andrew sounded content as he sat back in his seat. "You did it."

"Yes, we did." They were a team, and Samantha was grateful for it.

"Do you need me to divert to a closer facility?" Reese asked a few minutes later.

To veer off course to request an emergency standby landing was rare. Most pilots would rather push on to their scheduled destination. She wasn't surprised to discover Reese was the type of pilot who would do whatever was necessary for their patient.

"No, thanks. We can make it to Trinity." Samantha busied her hands with double-checking every connection, readjusting the medication rates, all in an effort to hide the fact that her hands were shaking. She wondered if Andrew had any idea how close their patient had come to dying.

"ETA twenty-five minutes." Reese's steady voice filled her helmet. "Just let me know if you need anything. I'm climbing back up another five hundred feet."

"Her pressure is dropping again," Andrew said, concern lacing his tone.

"I'm going to place a new line. I'm not convinced the one they put in is any good."

"What can I do?" This time, Andrew seemed determined to help rather than freak out.

"Prep the right side of her chest." She pulled out a new central line kit and sterile gloves.

"Dr. Kearn, do you need me to reduce altitude again?"

She was surprised to hear Reese address her so formally, but she was thankful he was paying attention to what was going on with their patient. The situation was still tenuous, but his reassuring voice remained her anchor.

"If you could." Somewhere along the way her fingers had stopped shaking and she was able to insert the needle and find the subclavian vein without difficulty. *That's it*, she told herself. *Just pretend you're in the ED where you completed months of training. See? No problem.*

Within minutes, she had the new line placed.

"Move the drips to the new line," she told Andrew. "I have good blood return. The chest X-ray will have to wait until we land."

Moments later, Jamie's blood pressure returned to normal. Satisfied, Samantha quickly cleaned and dressed the site.

"Sounds like things are better back there," Reese said.

She found herself smiling. "They are."

"ETA fifteen minutes. Less if I put more air under our belly. There's a nice tailwind up there."

The image of Reese body surfing, flying like Superman on a wave of wind, made her smile widen. Now that the worst was over, she could afford to relax.

"Sure, why not? I like a little air under my belly. And things are good back here."

Andrew made several notations in the medical record, then reduced the rate of the dopamine drip. With the line working properly, Jamie didn't need those massive doses she'd been on when they'd picked her up.

Something the ICU attending at the hospital should have figured out for himself.

She decided against pulling out the line that wasn't working, fearing that it would only cause uncontrolled bleeding. They were so focused on their patient that she didn't realize how much time had passed until she heard Reese's voice in her ear.

"Five minutes until landing."

"Thanks." Samantha helped Andrew prepare their patient for transport. She hit the button on her mic, signaling a call to the paramedic base. "Lifeline to paramedic base, please let Trinity's ICU staff know that we need a chest X-ray completed upon arrival. A new central line was placed in the right subclavian vein."

"Roger Lifeline."

Reese landed the helicopter with finesse on the rooftop helipad at Trinity Medical Center. Samantha waited until Reese gave them the all clear before jumping out to unload their patient.

As promised, the portable chest X-ray machine was waiting for them in the ICU. The digital reading proved that the line she'd placed was in the correct place and verified that the original line had gone through the vein. Even better, the air pocket in Jamie's lungs was already resolving.

Relieved, Samantha watched the ICU team work on Jamie, a woman only eight years her senior. Now that she'd handed over Jamie's care, the seriousness of the situation hit hard. This poor young woman had almost died up there. Thank heavens, she'd recognized the problem early enough to fix it.

"Nice job, Dr. Kearn." Andrew pulled the gurney out into the hall. "Ready to go?"

"Yeah." She wasn't really, but of course, her work here

was finished. She'd survived her first solo flight. Surely they'd get easier from here on out. Now, if only she could find a way to get the rest of her personal life on track.

One step at a time. You have a new apartment, and you've just about finished your training, only five more months to go. You finally have your independence. Be thankful for what you have.

Once they were back on the rooftop landing pad, she and Andrew headed over to where Reese waited with the chopper.

She frowned when she noticed that Reese had shut the machine down. He stood outside the helicopter, his expression grim as he stared at the aircraft.

"What's wrong?" Samantha asked.

"Ice on the blades. It's amazing we made it here in one piece. We'll have to de-ice before we can return to the Lifeline Air Rescue hangar."

REESE'S thigh muscles quivered with the effort of keeping himself upright as the bones in his legs seemingly disintegrated into dust. His face felt frozen, but he couldn't relax. He refused to let the rest of the crew know how badly this had shaken him.

They'd almost crashed.

In fact, he had no idea why they hadn't.

Red dots swam before his eyes until he feared he would end up much like the unconscious patient they'd just unloaded minutes earlier. He didn't want to believe what he'd seen, but the vision of the ice-covered blades was indelibly etched in his brain.

He'd noticed the slightest change in the stick as they'd

landed. He wanted to claim instinct had forced him to double-check the chopper blades, but in truth, he'd been following routine training that was drilled into every pilot.

Five minutes longer and they certainly would have crashed. Or at the very least been forced into a hard landing.

Was this how Valerie had felt in those moments before the crash? And Greg? Had his best friend noticed the slight hesitation of the stick mid-flight, or had the blades just stopped spinning?

Did he really want to know what had gone through his fiancée's and best friend's minds before they'd died?

The frankly curious gazes of Samantha and Andrew, watching as he de-iced the chopper, was all that kept him from sinking to his knees.

"Reese, do you need help?"

Samantha's lyrical sweet voice helped strengthen his resolve not to show his weakness. *Dr. Kearn to you, dummy,* he chided himself. The lady was smart, cool under pressure, and she deserved his respect, not his overly familiar thoughts. He didn't turn around but sensed rather than heard her come up behind him. A light evergreen scent teased his nostrils, kicking his pulse into high gear. The metallic taste of fear faded, quickly replaced by the slightest stirring of desire.

"No, thanks. I'll be finished in a few minutes." His voice sounded wooden to his ears, but hopefully Samantha wouldn't notice.

Dr. Kearn. Get it through your concrete-lined skull, she's Dr. Kearn!

"This is a first for me, being grounded to de-ice," she admitted softly, stepping into the line of his peripheral vision. "I guess it's better to be safe than sorry."

No, it was better to be safe than *dead*. The living were the only ones who were sorry. Reese mentally drew himself back on track. No sense in scaring the daylights out of the rest of the crew. Better that he kept his dark thoughts to himself.

"There, I'm finished." He verified the chemicals had performed their magic and pronounced the helicopter back in flying form. "I'll put this stuff away, then we can board."

"Reese?"

Bracing himself, he slowly turned to face her. For a moment he couldn't speak. She was so beautiful, no matter how hard she tried not to be. She'd caught his eye that very first day, her glorious red hair pulled into a no-nonsense braid and her creamy complexion free of makeup. She appeared oblivious to the male attention she drew from the other paramedics and physician crew members. Several pilots had commented about her, wondering about her availability, but Reese noticed that she never made a flirtatious gesture or remark. Almost as if she made it a point to never cross the line of polite friendliness. The "off-limits" signs couldn't have been any clearer.

Which was fine with him. He was happy enough to admire her from afar. She'd only be part of the Lifeline crew for another five months before she'd graduate to a full-fledged physician.

"Yes? What is it?" He pulled himself together with an effort.

"With the ice on the blades, how close were we to crashing?"

He hesitated, tempted to gloss over the risk, but decided he couldn't lie to her. It wasn't fair, not when her life had been on the line as much as his. "Too close."

"I see." Her eyebrows drew together to form a solemn line. "Thanks for telling me."

He nearly groaned. Why couldn't she just yell at him or something? He deserved that much. He was the captain of the ship. And he'd almost gotten her killed.

"Get your gear, we're ready to roll." His brusque response dimmed the sparkle in her eyes, but he told himself it was for the best. Theirs was a professional relationship, nothing more. He quickly stashed the supplies back in the hangar, then pulled the bird out of the shelter. Within moments, they were airborne once again.

The return ride was less than ten minutes, but there was an obvious lack of chatter amongst the crew as he set the helicopter on the ground. He gave Samantha and Andrew the signal to disembark, then shut down the engine.

Reese took a few extra moments to go through the basic post-flight checklist, then headed into the Lifeline lounge. Andrew and Samantha were standing there, along with some sort of delivery man holding a flower arrangement.

"Dr. Samantha Kearn?" the guy was asking as he stared down at his clipboard.

She didn't answer right away, forcing him to look up at her. "You're Dr. Samantha Kearn?" he repeated.

She nodded.

"Flower delivery for you, ma'am. Please sign here."

He thrust the clipboard at her, and she signed the form, a careful blankness in her normally expressive gray eyes. Reese frowned. What was this about? Most women were thrilled with surprise gifts, but Samantha looked green as if she might throw up.

"Wow, Dr. Kearn, someone loves you," Andrew teased. "Who is it from? Hey, there isn't a card."

The tiny hairs on the back of Reese's neck lifted in alarm. The delivery man thrust the cellophane-wrapped flower at her, but Samantha quickly pulled her hands away, stumbling backward out of reach. When she regained her footing, she gestured to the table. "No, ah, set it there, please."

There was something wrong with this picture. Reese recognized pure fright when he saw it. In fact, Samantha looked as awful as he'd felt when he'd seen the ice coating the chopper blades.

"Andrew, did you file the flight paperwork yet?" He pinned the paramedic with a pointed look.

Andrew shook his head. "No, but I will."

"Good. I have my report here, too. Let's get these finished."

Andrew took the not too subtle hint and obediently left the lounge. Reese followed more slowly. At the doorway, he hesitated, then turned to walk back inside, just in time to see Samantha gingerly pick up the flower, still encased in plastic wrap and hurl it into the metal trash can in the corner. A loud crash reverberated through the room.

Definitely, something wrong.

"Who sent it?" Reese asked softly. He wasn't just being nosy, he could feel Samantha's tension all the way across the room. He suddenly wanted to protect her from whoever was bothering her.

She spun around to face him, swallowed hard, then squared her shoulders, bravely meeting his gaze. "There wasn't a card."

"Still, you know who sent it, don't you?"

She remained stubbornly silent, but the guilty flash and abrupt lowering of her eyes was answer enough.

2

Sam froze, caught by the imploring gaze of Reese's dark eyes. She knew he was waiting for her to tell what she knew, but she didn't want to admit her past failures out loud, and especially not to the handsome chopper pilot.

During the flight, she felt connected to Reese, as if their minds were completely in sync, each instinctively working together to bring Jamie safely to Trinity. He'd helped her as much as Andrew had, maybe more. She knew Reese deserved part of the credit for making her first solo flight a resounding success.

But when she returned to the hangar and found the lily, her brief euphoria had faded, replaced by a sick clenching in her gut. Dennis Markowitz, her controlling ex-husband, had found her again. She'd once loved lilies, until Dennis had showered her with them over and over again. Now the very scent of a lily made her feel sick.

They'd been divorced for six months and separated longer than that. Why did he persist in seeking ways to make her life miserable?

Because he can, she silently admitted. *Because I let him, by overreacting to his childish gestures.* In a few months, she'd graduate and take her emergency medicine boards to become an attending physician. How was it that the minute Dennis pulled one of his stunts, she felt hopelessly trapped in his manipulations?

Self-doubt seeped through her mind. Maybe Dennis was right. Maybe she'd never make it alone.

As quickly as the thought came, she shoved it away. She was strong. She could do this.

"You know who sent it, don't you?"

Since Reese was still looking at her expectantly, she forced herself to answer. "No, I don't." She kept her expression carefully blank, hoping Reese wouldn't notice her hands were shaking.

"Sure, you do. It's okay, I understand."

His matter-of-fact statement caught her off guard. She fought the urge to confess. Usually, she could keep one step ahead of prying questions. She certainly had more than enough practice at hiding the truth.

She strove to sound casual. "Doesn't matter. Past history." Holding his gaze wasn't easy. Nearly six feet tall and broad-shouldered, Reese was the strong, silent type. He didn't talk about himself much, but he had a knack for drawing out confidences from others.

One look from his melt-your-heart chocolate-brown eyes and she'd nearly blabbed the truth.

For a long moment, he simply waited. His intent expression spoke volumes, basically telling her he knew she was lying and was debating whether or not to call her on it. Finally, he nodded.

"I'm here for you, if you need anything. You can always call me."

"Sure thing." She released her breath in a soundless sigh. Not that she planned to seek him out, but if she did choose to confide in him, what would his reaction be? Would Reese look down at her for being divorced? Or would he understand her desperation to be free from her husband's overly controlling nature? As a woman in a male-dominated profession, she knew only too well how the male species stuck together.

Reese turned away, then glanced back over his shoulder. "Dr. Kearn?"

His formal address almost made her wince. So much for feeling as if they were true partners in flight. He didn't use titles when he spoke with any of the others, so it couldn't be by accident that he'd singled her out. "Yes?"

"If you really don't want any more deliveries, let security know. We take our safety very seriously around here."

Samantha stared after his retreating figure. Did he think she would do anything to harm the crew?

Dennis wanted to control her, to convince her to come back to him, not to physically hurt her. Reese didn't have to act as if she was a total safety risk.

Some of her anger evaporated, though, because she knew Reese only cared about keeping them safe. And she hadn't told Reese the truth, so how could he know Dennis's intent? Besides, the way Dennis had found her at Lifeline was creepy. She hadn't heard from him in two months, so why now? Should she make plans to move out of her new apartment? Quit her Lifeline rotation? She could only imagine what Dr. Ben Harris, her boss and the medical director of Trinity's emergency department, would think about that.

Endless questions rattled in her brain like a box of uncooked noodles. Now that Dennis had found her, he wasn't likely to just simply leave her alone. Maybe she should call the police and tell them about the lily. After the divorce, she had taken out a restraining order against Dennis, for all the good it did. She crossed the room toward the phone, then stopped. There wasn't a card, which meant they wouldn't be able to prove Dennis had sent the flower. Oh, they'd investigate the flower shop where the delivery had originated, but she'd been down that road before. No doubt the transaction had been made with cash, and if Dennis had run true to form, he'd found someone else to do his dirty work, ensuring there would be no tracing the lily to him.

The one thing Dennis excelled at was covering his tracks.

Samantha gave herself a mental shake. Better to stop dwelling on Dennis the Menace. Agonizing over his next move played right into his psycho scheme. She detested his ability to intrude on her thoughts.

Abruptly she straightened and squared her shoulders. What was she worried about? She was a free and independent woman, not the naïve person who had married too young. It was about time Dennis realized the truth.

She was determined to remain immune to his mind games.

Despite her determination to forget her past, the heavy, cloying scent of the lily seemed to follow her as she restocked the supplies they'd used from the flight bag. She was glad to be alone, away from Reese's all too knowing brown eyes. What she wouldn't give for a call out now. Something to occupy her mind would be heavenly.

"Hungry?" Reese asked from the doorway of the supply room.

She snapped her head around. Already, her muscles were tighter than a coiled spring. She let her breath out in a soundless sigh. "Ah, sure. Give me a few minutes."

Reese waited patiently for her to finish. His silent presence was overwhelmingly close, and her fingers turned clumsy, nearly dropping a small stack of catheters on the floor.

She managed to get them packed into the flight bag, then double-checked to make sure she had everything. "I'll put this away and meet you in the lounge."

"I'll take it for you." He easily slid the bag from her grasp.

Logic told her Reese was simply being polite, but his take-charge manner rubbed her the wrong way. Plus, she couldn't help but wonder if he didn't trust her near the helicopter. She'd noticed over the past few weeks how Reese watched Mitch the mechanic like a hawk while he worked on it. The other crew members teased Reese about it, although he didn't seem to care. And hadn't his reaction to the iced blades been a little strange? Surely, as a pilot, he'd been forced to de-ice choppers before.

Of course, the danger had been very real. He'd admitted as much when she'd asked him point-blank.

Normally she didn't think about the danger of flying any more than ambulance drivers probably considered the threat of a potential crash while they raced to an accident scene. The helicopter was just a means of transport, one she happened to prefer. And the Lifeline had an excellent twenty-five-year cash-free history.

She was just being paranoid. Reese took his responsibilities seriously. So seriously, she wondered about him sometimes. During these past few weeks, she couldn't remember ever hearing him laugh out loud. But Reese's somber attitude wasn't her concern. She couldn't afford to worry about him. Her goal was to graduate and to move on with her own life, in that order.

Andrew joined her in the lounge. A few minutes later, Reese strode in.

"What are you hungry for? Take-out pizza or the deli across the street?" Reese asked

Samantha was about to suggest the pizza until she realized it was her way of avoiding going outside because she feared seeing Dennis. *Don't do this*, she warned herself. *Don't let him force you into hiding from life. This is all part of his need for control.*

"The deli," she quickly spoke up before she could change her mind.

Andrew grinned and rubbed his hands together. "Yeah, I'm in the mood for a Reuben sandwich."

She felt Reese's gaze on her but tried to ignore it as they grabbed their thick quilted Lifeline jackets. The frigid Wisconsin winter wind was sharp enough to etch steel. Reese gestured for them to precede him out the door. Sam kept her gaze forward as they crossed the street, refusing to search for signs of Dennis following her.

The deli was packed with people, even on such a cold day. They were close enough that, if a call came in, they'd still be able to get into the air within the designated five-minute time frame. They stood in line and placed their orders, then waited another few minutes until their food was ready. Samantha only hoped she'd have time to finish her turkey sandwich before the next call came in.

While the noisy deli was hardly an intimate atmosphere, she was keenly aware of the slightest brush of Reese's knee against hers as the three of them sat around a small table. When his knee stayed warmly against hers, she waited for him to move. When he didn't, she subtly shifted away. Concentrating on her food, she knew she was being ridiculous. No doubt Reese hadn't even noticed the innocent touch.

"I still can't believe you inserted a chest tube in flight," Andrew gushed around a mouthful of his corned beef sandwich. "That was totally awesome."

Reese raised a brow. "Is a chest tube such an unusual procedure?"

Sam shrugged. "Not really. It's pretty commonplace in the emergency department." Andrew's praise made her uncomfortable. Secretly she had been worried during the procedure, but Reese's calm voice had helped keep her fingers steady.

"I've been at Lifeline for three years, and I haven't seen it done until today," Andrew stubbornly persisted.

Sam ate her turkey and tomato sandwich but could feel Reese's intense gaze on her, silently agreeing with Andrew's assessment.

At least her medical skills were something to be proud of, not like her personal life. There, she was a complete failure.

The morose thoughts caused her appetite to evaporate. She crumpled her napkin and tossed it on her half-eaten food. "I'm finished, so I'm heading back."

Before she could stand, Reese's hand clasped her arm. She caught her breath at his touch. His fingers were warm, holding her securely but nowhere near hard enough to bruise. "Wait. Don't go alone."

The urge to pull away and stomp out of there was strong. Instinctively, she bristled. Who is he to tell her what to do?

"I'm fine. Really." She flashed him a reassuring smile. "Please?"

His quiet plea stopped her from leaving as nothing else would have. Dennis had never asked, he'd demanded. She knew most men weren't like her ex, but somehow her first reaction was to lash out as if they were.

"I guess I can wait." She settled back into her seat.

"Thank you." Reese stared at her for a moment, then slowly withdrew his hand from her arm.

She almost stroked the spot where he touched her, amazed at the strange, tingling sensation left by his warm palm. Normally her skin crawled when a man touched her. What had changed? Why didn't she have the same reaction with Reese Jarvis?

She couldn't come up with a good answer as the guys finished their meals and in record time, no doubt virtually inhaling their food on her behalf, just so she wouldn't have to wait.

Guilt returned to full force. "Don't rush. It's not as if we have calls waiting," she urged them.

"We're not rushing, are we?" Reese asked Andrew after swallowing his last bit of food.

"Nope. I always eat fast, drives my wife nuts," Andrew cheerfully replied.

She gave up as they quickly rolled their wrappers into balls and stood to leave.

Outside, Reese and Andrew fell into step on either side of her as they walked back to the Lifeline hangar. Sam was struck by how hyperaware she was of Reese on her right, while Andrew could've been nonexistent on her left. The faintest whiff of Reese's spicy aftershave enticed her to move closer.

What was wrong with her? Reese certainly seemed like a

nice guy, but heaven knew, she'd been wrong before. She didn't have time for this weird attraction. Not when she needed all her energy to focus on finishing her residency and getting her personal life on track.

She would follow Reese's example and keep a professional distance between them. Which shouldn't be too difficult, especially since during their flight time Reese sat in the cockpit while she was in back caring for patients.

If she could only get his husky voice out of her head, she'd be fine.

REESE STARED BLINDLY at the weather radar screen. Even the icy blades were a distant memory. The strange flower delivery Samantha had received nagged at him, wreaking havoc with his concentration.

Surely it was just the idea that she might be in trouble, rather than the woman herself, that bothered him.

"Reese?"

He glanced up, startled to find the woman occupying his thoughts standing in front of him. Samantha—or rather Dr. Kearn— looked incredibly tiny in the navy blue figure-hugging flight suit. Too small to hold her own against some creep bugging her with a stupid gift.

"I want you to know I called security."

He was surprised at her blunt admission. The way she'd refused to tell him the truth earlier had him betting she wouldn't have continued to deny anything was wrong. A surge of anger about the situation caught him off guard. Who in the world had sent the thing to her anyway? And why didn't she just tell the creep to shove off? "Good. I'm glad."

"So there's no need to worry about a security breach." Samantha's gaze bored to his for a moment, then she gestured to the screen. "How much longer before the snow clears?"

"Not sure. Another hour at least." Reese frowned when she returned to leave. "Wait a minute, I wasn't implying you had caused a breach in security."

"Weren't you?" Her cool tone flayed him. She spun on her heel and stalked away.

Reese stared after her, then dropped his head into his hand. Man, he'd really botched that one. He never intended to hurt her, but maybe it was better she stayed ticked at him. Her slender arm had felt far too good beneath his hand. Listening to her lilting voice through the headset in flight was bad enough. Every word she spoke made him think of warm fires and endless winter nights. Being so close to her was tempting.

He never should have touched her.

He'd watched many like her come and go. Senior emergency medicine residents did the required rotations, then left to graduate as full-fledged physicians. The only full-time doctor on staff was Dr. Jared O'Connor, and he was a pediatric specialist as well as the medical director of the Lifeline Air Rescue program.

Watching residents rotate through had never bothered him before, especially the women. He wasn't in the market for a relationship. *Ever.* The pain of losing someone you loved was too devastating. Didn't he see the same theme over and over again with every injured or sick person they transported? Every patient had someone who mourned the potential loss of a wife, a father, a sister, or a child. He'd been down that road before and had no intention of repeating the experience.

More than enough reason to remind himself that the beautiful Dr. Kearn was off-limits.

A call came in, requesting response to a crash scene. Samantha materialized in the doorway before he'd finished reading the entire message on his pager.

"Ready to go?"

"I don't think so." Reese gestured to the radar screen. "The snow is getting thick and heavy. The higher the altitude, the more likely the snow will be freezing rain. Temperatures are hovering around freezing. Dangerous flying weather."

Her frown was perplexed. "But we've flown in snow before."

Reese hesitated for a moment, then shrugged. He knew there were pilots who pushed the line of safe flying, but he wasn't one of them. Snow in and of itself didn't justify red flying conditions, but freezing rain did, and the temperature was too fickle right now to make the distinction.

Swallowing his own disappointment, he picked up the phone to call the paramedic base. "Base, we're in yellow flying conditions that are leaning toward red. I don't think we should respond to this call."

"Roger, will notify the paramedic unit closest to the scene."

Samantha stared at him for a long minute, and he braced himself for the arguments he could practically see dancing in her head. To his surprise, though, she simply turned and left.

Guilt weighed heavy on his heart. There was only an hour left until the end of their twelve-hour shift, and Reese reminded himself how keeping the crew safe was his top priority. The crash victims would get the aid they needed through ground transport. Still, he silently admitted that he didn't like turning down anyone in distress. Their purpose was to save lives, but he knew from painful firsthand experience that he couldn't save anyone by putting the entire crew at risk.

The weather had been similar, thick wet swirling snow, the night Greg and Valerie had crashed. He had tortured himself for weeks after their deaths, wondering if he could have prevented it. Reese had switched shifts with Greg so he could take his grandmother to her doctor appointment. Greg had been his friend, but Greg had also been known for being a risky flyer. Greg had been arrogant, thinking his skills at the stick had far outweighed the threat from the weather.

Had Valerie been willing to go along, or had she tried to get Greg to call off the flight? Reese had no way of knowing the truth. He could only comfort himself with the knowledge that Valerie had loved being a flight nurse and had accepted the risks just like the rest of them.

He didn't realize how long he'd been staring morosely at the radar screen until the pilot coming on shift, Nate, strode into the debriefing room. "Hey, Reese. How's the weather?"

"I've seen better." Reese subtly glanced at his watch. Surprise widened his eyes. Where had the last hour gone?

"Are we in the red?"

"Yellow, but I turned down a scene call a while ago." Reese glanced over Nate's shoulder. "When the rest of the crew arrives, I'll fill you in."

Within five minutes, Kate and another senior resident, Dr. Zane Taylor, entered the debriefing room. Reese quickly gave them an update on the ice incident and the impact of the weather conditions. Samantha and Andrew briefed them on the transport they had done earlier that day, including the placement of the chest tube. Kate and Zane were impressed by Samantha's quick thinking. She flushed and averted her gaze, obviously uncomfortable with the attention.

Many of the physicians were a bit on the arrogant side, a fact he readily accepted. He'd always figured you had to be a tad arrogant to work in such a stressful job, and truthfully, pilots were similar in many ways. Samantha was different, and he couldn't help but wonder if the mystery guy who had sent the flower was part of the reason she didn't like being the center of attention.

Reese purposefully waited until she and Andrew left the debriefing room before adding another portion of his report, one he preferred to give out of Dr. Kearn's earshot.

"Security has been instructed not to accept any gifts of any nature for Dr. Kearn," he confided.

"Gifts?" Kate's eyes widened. "Why ever not? I'd love for someone to send me gifts."

Reese frowned. "Maybe, but I don't think Dr. Kearn's gift was a token of appreciation. The details aren't any of our business."

"They are if there's a threat involved," Nate argued.

"A flower isn't exactly a threat." Reese lifted a hand to hold another argument. "I'll let Jared know, although I'm certain Dr. Kearn will take care of that, too. Still, for now, just make a notation in the book that no deliveries are to be accepted on behalf of Dr. Kearn."

Nate muttered under his breath but reluctantly agreed. Reese grabbed his coat and left the hangar.

Being a weekend, there weren't many cars in the parking lot, especially at 1930 in the evening. Darkness had fallen, but the fresh white snow covering the ground glittered like shards of glass in the moonlight. Reese blinked through the swirling snowflakes, noticing how the wheels of a large dark-colored Oldsmobile spun uselessly in the snow. Since Andrew drove a minivan, he figured Samantha was behind the wheel.

"Hey!" He waved to get Samantha's attention and hastened over to tap on her window. "I have a truck. Why don't you let me drive you home?"

She rolled down the window. "No thanks, I'm fine."

"Come on, the streets are bound to be slippery, and I have a four-wheel drive. No reason to have two cars on the road."

"Look, Reese, I don't need your help. Thanks anyway." Even as she spoke, she stamped hard on the accelerator and the ancient Oldsmobile lurched forward as the wheels caught pavement.

Reese stood in the snow, staring after her as she drove off, trying to understand why the slightest offer of help was apparently unwelcome by the beautiful yet reticent flight doctor.

3
___

Samantha rested her forehead on top of the steering wheel and uttered a low groan. Things had happened so fast she didn't even remember sliding into the ditch. Stupid bunny just had to hop into the middle of the road. She'd swerved to avoid hitting it and had ended up with her rear tire stuck in the ditch for her efforts.

Yep. Reese had been right. The roads were slick.

She sighed, lifted her head, and tried rocking her car out of the ditch again. No dice. She was good and stuck.

No use dwelling on the situation. At least she wasn't too far from the Oak Terrace apartment building where she lived. The walk would do her good. The only hassle would be getting to work in the morning without a car.

She opened her door and watched a big black truck pull alongside her. For a moment, her heart raced with fear, until she recognized Reese's concerned face peering at her through his open passenger window.

"Are you all right?"

"Just dandy." Sam braced herself for the *I told you so* he was bound to say.

"Will you allow me to give you a ride home? Or would you rather I try to push your car out of the ditch?"

Surprised, she stared at him. He was giving her a choice? Without trying to tell her how idiotic she was to drive into the ditch in the first place? How refreshing.

"I have to work early in the morning, so I'd really like to get my car out, if you don't mind."

He nodded, seemingly not surprised by her request. "I don't mind. I'll park up ahead, then push you out."

Sam was grateful he didn't give her a lecture or rub in how foolish she was. She had a feeling Reese wouldn't have swerved for a bunny, or if he had, his four-wheel-drive truck would never have ended up in the ditch. True to his word, he trudged past her open driver side window to the back of her car, checking where her wheels had slid off the road.

"Do you know how to rock the car?" His gaze mirrored his doubt.

"Yes."

"Good. Start rocking and I'll give you a push." His voice grew muffled as he made his way to the back of the car. In her rearview mirror, she saw that he was braced along the bumper behind the passenger side rear wheel, giving her a nod to indicate he was ready.

"Here goes," she muttered. She hit the gas intermittently, setting up a rocking motion. Once. Twice. Three times. Four.

Without warning, her tire caught hold and her car shot up the embankment onto the road, and she quickly hit the brakes.

Reese scrambled up after her, then jumped into the passenger seat of her car. The Olds was almost eighteen years old, and many of its features, like the automatic locks, had stopped working a long time ago.

She cranked up the heat for his benefit, then turned to him, flashing a warm smile. "Thanks, Reese. I really appreciate your help."

"You're welcome. For a minute there I thought you were planning to walk home. Do you live far from here?"

"No. About a mile or two down the road in the Oak Terrace apartments."

"Really?" His eyebrows shot up in surprise. "Me, too."

Reese lived in the same complex? She'd never seen him around, but then again, she'd only lived there for a couple of months. "Which building?"

"The south building."

"Oh, I live in the north building." Which probably explained why she hadn't seen him yet. The news that Reese lived so close didn't alarm her. Instead, a flicker of excitement danced along her nerves. Now that she knew he lived nearby, basically within walking distance, she'd drive yourself crazy watching for him.

An awkward silence fell between them. He didn't make an effort to get out of her car, and Sam wasn't sure what she should do. She didn't feel right kicking him out of her car after he had gone to such trouble of pushing her out of the ditch. But what on earth was he waiting for?

"Do you mind if I ask a personal question?"

Her gut clenched in warning. "No, I guess not."

His hair was damp from the melting snow, and he slanted her a sideways glance. "Are you married?"

"No!" Cheeks burning with mortification, she couldn't believe he'd thought she was married. Samantha knew she didn't owe him an explanation but found herself telling him anyway. "I'm divorced."

The relief in his expression nearly made her smile. Then

his brows pulled together in a dark frown. "Is your ex-husband the one who'd sent the flower?"

She supposed it was an easy guess. What was the point of denying it? Reluctantly, she nodded. "He's persistent."

"What's his name?" There was a hint of steel in his tone.

"Dennis Markowitz."

"How long have you been divorced?"

Sam shifted in her seat. "Six months."

"More than persistent, then."

She couldn't argue, but Dennis was the last person she wanted to talk about. He was the past, and her goal was to focus on the future. The hour was getting late, and she really did have to work in the morning. "Well, thanks again. Did you want me to drive you home?"

"Huh?" Reese glanced around as if he'd forgotten he was still sitting in her car. "Oh, no. But wait for me and I'll follow you."

Before she could respond one way or the other, he opened the door and climbed from the car.

Sam swallowed a protest, watching as he hunched his shoulders against the cold wind and headed for his truck. He didn't need to follow her home, but since they were going the same way, there wasn't any point in arguing.

Besides, her pulse still hadn't settled back to normal after he'd asked if she was married. Had he simply been fishing for information on who'd sent the lily? Or had he wanted to know her marital status for personal reasons?

When he flashed his lights, she pulled out into the nonexistent traffic ahead of him. Reese's truck lights were reassuringly bright behind her.

Despite her vow to concentrate on her career, on forgetting the mistakes in her past, Sam found herself secretly hoping Reese had asked about her marital status for personal reasons.

The ride home was a short one. She pulled into an empty parking space in front of her north building, fully expecting Reese to continue on. But he surprised her by parking his truck beside her car.

She climbed from the Oldsmobile, glancing over as he did the same. "What are you doing?"

"I thought I'd walk you inside." Reese slammed his truck door behind him.

"There's no reason to walk me in," she protested.

"Hey, humor me, will you?" Reese fell into step beside her. "What's the harm?"

Sam shrugged, unable to think of a reason not to. He was certainly going out of his way to be nice. Too bad she wasn't in the market for a man. She shot him a quick look as they headed up the sidewalk. Did he think she was? In the market for a man?

Her boots slid in the slippery snow, and he quickly cupped a hand under her elbow. "Easy, don't fall."

She wanted to point out that she was already falling, the ground seemingly disappearing from beneath her feet. Every time Reese touched her, she was free-falling into new territory. Having Reese's undivided attention was a completely disarming experience. One that shifted her off balance.

She used her key to access the building. Once inside, Reese paused in front of the elevator. "Which floor?"

"Ground level." She brushed past him to unlock the second door. One of the reasons she liked this apartment building was because of the decent security system.

"This way." She turned left and headed down the hall to

her apartment. Outside the door, she turned and forced a smile. "This is it. Thanks for walking me in."

"No problem."

When he didn't immediately leave, she raised a brow. Now what? "Are you planning to follow me inside?"

"Just enough to make sure there are no unwelcome surprises." Reese's expression never changed, but she thought his eyes darkened.

"I'm sure Dennis didn't deliver a lily here." When Reese didn't budge, she suppressed a sigh and unlocked her door. She opened it with one hand, finding and switching on the lights with the other. A quick sweeping glance confirmed there was nothing out of order.

"See? Everything's fine." She stepped back against the door, gesturing for him to look for himself.

Reese nodded again and stepped closer, craning his neck to see the inside of her apartment. She caught another whiff of his spicy aftershave and shrank back against the door to stop from throwing herself into his arms. Dear heaven, what was wrong with her? Reese was just being nice. Was she so unaccustomed to nice behavior from a man that she couldn't recognize it for what it was?

It was a sad testament to her messed up personal life.

"Thanks again, Reese. See you tomorrow." She injected cheerfulness into her tone to hide her confusion. Taking several side steps, she eased along the door heading into her apartment. Reese didn't have to do anything more than stand there and look at her to crumble her instinctive resistance toward the male species.

His gaze met hers, and time hung suspended between them. He was very close, his eyes dark, wide, and intent. For a moment, she wondered if he might lean forward and kiss her. Her lips parted in anticipation. If he did, would she be brave enough to kiss him back?

"Good night, Samantha." His voice was low, husky, drawing out the syllables of her full name in a rumbling tone. Dazed and breathless, she realized he'd used her full name. Samantha. No more Dr. Kearn, she was Samantha now. "See you tomorrow."

Speechless, she could only stare after him as he turned and ambled away. Realizing she was standing with the door wide open, staring down an empty hallway, she quickly closed and locked it, then leaned against the wood, her head tilted back against the door, her heart beating rapidly in her chest.

Reese wasn't a part of her master plan, but somehow, she suspected he wasn't going to be easy to ignore.

IThe thought brought a thrill of anticipation she hadn't experienced in years.

~

THE SNOW WAS FALLING in thick, swirling flakes as Reese headed outside toward his truck. Reese lifted his face, the snow a welcome coolness against his flushed skin.

Man, he needed to get a grip. He'd called her Samantha. He liked her name, but that wasn't the point. What happened to Dr. Kearn? She was supposed to stay Dr. Kearn. How could he keep her out of his head now that he called her Samantha?

Reese drove around Samantha's building to his assigned parking space. He shut off the engine and got out of the truck and then locked the doors. Trudging through the snow, he didn't notice the sharp wind in his face. Inside the building, he headed to his apartment.

The layout was an exact replica of Samantha's, only he was on the second floor. As he threw his keys on the kitchen table, he wondered how she was doing. After the day she'd had, she deserved to relax.

He found himself wondering what she did to relax, then gave himself a mental head-slap.

What in the world was wrong with him?

Samantha's personal life wasn't his business. Yet, she'd gotten to him, despite how she'd clearly tried to avoid telling him anything. In fact, he was rather ticked about how he'd had to drag information from her. He hadn't imagined the instant flare of panic in her eyes when he'd pulled up beside her car while being stuck in the ditch.

So, Samantha liked her privacy. Big deal. Did he really blame her? He understood how she felt. He hadn't announced his miserable past for everyone at Lifeline to lament over.

Valerie. With a guilty start, Reese realized he hadn't really thought about his late fiancée at all since earlier that day. And even then, only because the ice on his blades had reminded him of the crash. For a moment, he tried to imagine Valerie's tanned features, her easy smile, but instead, Samantha emerged from the mist of his memory. Samantha's creamy skin, her red hair pulled into that no-nonsense braid, her tentative smile.

The shadow of fear in her eyes.

Today was the anniversary of Valerie's and Greg's deaths. Yet somehow being with Samantha had managed to obliterate his sadness and regret. There wasn't anything he could do to help Valerie now, but he could help Samantha feel safe during the remaining months of her Lifeline rotation.

At least until she graduated from her residency and moved on somewhere far away, maybe even in another state.

Far enough that he would be able to forget about her once and for all.

4

Reese left his apartment to head to work early, but he was disappointed to note that Samantha's ancient vehicle was already missing from her parking spot. They should carpool to work since they lived so close.

He winced at the insane thought. Who was he trying to kid? He didn't give a hoot about saving fuel; it wasn't as if the Oak Terrace apartment complex was far from Lifeline. No, what he really wanted was an excuse to spend more time with Samantha.

Stupid to dream up ways to spend more time with her. They were scheduled to fly together often enough as it was. Sleep had been a long time in coming last night, thanks to his overactive imagination. He'd woken feeling groggy, aching for something he couldn't have.

Inside the Lifeline hangar, he found Samantha standing in the debriefing room. He could've used a crowbar to pry his tongue from the roof of his mouth when he saw her. Her fresh, clean beauty literally took his breath away. There was nothing spectacular about the regulation navy blue flight suit she wore, but she'd left the zipper open a few inches, revealing the white turtleneck beneath. The material almost entirely covered her skin, but for some reason, on her, the white turtleneck sweater was incredibly alluring.

"Good morning," he finally managed.

"Hello, Reese." Her brief smile was gone before he had a chance to fully appreciate it. He tried to think of something to say that might bring it back.

Mentally, he gave a snort. Enough already. He and Samantha were flight partners, nothing more. Time to get back on friendship footing. "So, how's the weather?" This was one time when talking about the weather wasn't inane chatter but pertinent to the job they were paid to do.

"Clear skies. You are good to go," Nate piped up from his seat beside the radar screen.

"Great. Then we don't need to refuse any calls," Samantha replied.

Reese raised a brow at her irritable tone. "I don't like refusing calls either."

"I know." For a moment she looked chagrined. "But there's nothing worse than feeling helpless. At least we know that today if something comes in, we can respond." She glanced at Nate. "Are there any transfers waiting in the wings?"

"Nope." Nate shook his head.

Reese took off his jacket and carried it into the small pilot's room adjacent to the debriefing area. He mulled over Samantha's words as he hung up his jacket behind the door. None of them liked being grounded, Samantha had mentioned feeling helpless. A leftover emotion from her marriage to Markowitz? She hadn't confided the details of her breakup, but he desperately wanted to know more. Had her ex-husband made her feel helpless? Had he used his strength against her?

Anger simmered at the thought, but he reined himself in with an effort. His imagination was working overtime again. Just because Samantha hated feeling helpless, that didn't mean there was physical abuse in her past.

Besides, a guy who was abusive probably wouldn't bother sending flowers. Right? Right. He grimaced at the way he'd jumped to conclusions.

But what was the deal with the lily?

Shaking his head at the insatiable curiosity, Reese made his way back into the debriefing area. His pager went off simultaneously with Samantha's.

"Motor vehicle crash on the interstate, one adult victim in critical condition," he read the page out loud. He glanced at Samantha. "Where's Andrew? Are you ready to go?"

"He's getting coffee, but it can wait. We're ready."

Reese walked behind Samantha, the faint evergreen scent teasing his nostrils. What did she do, shower with the Christmas tree every morning? Don't go there. Imagining Samantha in the shower, with or without a Christmas tree, wasn't smart. He needed a clear mind to focus on flying.

"Andrew, come on. We have a transport," Samantha called as they passed the lounge. With obvious reluctance, the young paramedic set his freshly poured coffee aside and followed them out to the hangar.

All three of them grabbed helmets, then Reese headed for the chopper while Samantha and Andrew double-checked the flight bag of medical supplies. First, Reese open the hangar door, then using the triangular rolling base, he pushed the lightweight helicopter outside into the frigid air.

Samantha and Andrew quickly followed, jumping into

the helicopter through the side doors with the flight bag in tow.

Reese climbed into the cockpit and gently plugged in his headset so he wouldn't miss one minute of listening to Samantha's sweet voice.

Oh yeah. He had it bad.

With a resigned shake of his head, he started the engine. The crash scene wasn't far, just to the south about twenty miles. He communicated with the paramedic base, then told the rest of the crew to prepare for takeoff.

Samantha and Andrew were quiet in the back, and he wondered what they were thinking. Maybe Andrew was still half asleep, since he hadn't gotten his daily dose of caffeine. Reese stared down at the ribbon of highway below, taking note of the glaring sunlight from the east. He'd need to land in such a way as to avoid having the full force of the sun in his eyes on takeoff.

The mangled cars and rescue vehicles at the scene of the crash were visible from his vantage point in the air. Cueing his mic, he alerted Samantha and Andrew.

"ETA four minutes."

"Roger. We can see the crash site." Samantha's lyrical voice caused his gut to tighten with awareness. He forced himself to concentrate on power lines in choosing the best place to land. It was a large grassy field on the west side of the highway, where most of the debris from the crash was scattered. From the looks of things, the victims were in the field as well. He decided there was enough room for him to land on the empty portion of the field, close but not too close to the scene. He gently set down the chopper, then flipped the switch, dropping the rotation of the blades to their lowest setting.

"You're clear to go," he told them.

Through his window, Reese watched Andrew and Samantha exit the helicopter. He held his breath when they opened the back hatch and pulled out the gurney, the tail of the chopper being the most dangerous. In moments he saw them running alongside the gurney as they wheeled it over to the crash site. Sitting in the cockpit while the crew attended to the victims was the hardest part of his job. The pilot's responsibility was to stay with the bird. He understood the rules. You never knew if there was some wacko that would try to jump into an empty helicopter if left unattended. Still, understanding the rules didn't mean he had to like them.

The sun glinted brightly in the fiery hue of Samantha's hair. She and Andrew knelt beside a female victim, and Reese noticed the paramedic was holding back a man who appeared to be trying to get to the woman's side.

Her boyfriend? Husband? He couldn't be certain, but the frank anguish on the man's features reminded him of the day he received the phone call about Valerie and Greg's crash. The pain of losing someone you loved was indescribable.

Samantha and Andrew had already placed the victim on a gurney and seemed to be getting ready to bring her to the helicopter. Reese was glad. Their actions meant the woman was still alive, still had a chance at survival. He tapped his foot impatiently as he waited for them to approach.

The paramedic still held onto the guy who Reese could only assume had been in the crash with the woman. Samantha and Andrew had almost reached the helicopter when the guy broke loose from the paramedic's grip.

What was he doing? Reese shut down the engines as the guy ran straight for the gurney. He yanked off his helmet, pushed open the door, and jumped to the ground. He dashed toward Samantha and Andrew who looked up at the suddenly quiet chopper in surprise.

"Look out," he shouted.

The distraught man grabbed the woman on the gurney, nearly knocking Samantha to the ground with the force of his lunge. "Becky!" the guy cried. "No! She can't die! Becky!"

Reese grabbed the guy's arm before he could dislodge any of the lifesaving medical equipment Samantha may have connected to the patient. "Hey, buddy, you're not helping us here. She needs medical attention. We need to get her to the hospital as soon as possible."

"I'm coming with you." The guy was strong, and Reese had to dig his boot heels into the earth to prevent himself from being tossed aside. "Let me go!"

"Knock it off," he warned. He didn't want to toss the guy to the ground, but he would if he had to.

"You can't come along," Samantha said, regret shadowing her eyes as she held firmly onto the gurney. "I'm sorry, but I promise we'll take good care of her."

"I'm coming!" The guy yanked hard against the hold Reese had on him. "Becky, don't worry, hon. I'm coming with you."

Reese wrestled the guys grip off the gurney, then met Samantha's gaze over his head. "Get her into the chopper, quick."

Samantha and Andrew ran with the gurney toward the rear hatch door. Reese hoped the paramedics were on their way to help him subdue the man, or they'd never be able to get off the ground without him trying something stupid like jumping on for a ride.

A guy like this could cause them to crash.

Luckily, the paramedic saw what was happening and came to the rescue.

"Whoa, Jake, what are you doing?" One of them got in front of the man while the other helped Reese hang on to his arms. "You're not helping Becky, she needs to get to the hospital, fast."

The two paramedics worked together to force Jake to the ground. Once he was down, Reese was able to relinquish his hold on him.

"Keep him down until we're gone," he tersely advised.

The paramedics nodded their agreement. The one who'd been holding on to Jake earlier added, "He's not injured that we can see, but we'll probably have to sedate him and transport him to Trinity anyway."

"Good luck with that." Reese dashed to the helicopter and climbed into the cockpit.

Samantha and Andrew were already safely inside with their patient. Without wasting time, Reese quickly buckled in, pulled on his helmet, and notified the base they were lifting off. It took him a moment to get the engines back up and running, and he hoped that during the brief time they were stopped ice hadn't coated the blades. That was one of the reasons he kept the blades rotating, even when on the ground.

When he had rotors going at the appropriate speed, he guided the helicopter off the ground, keeping a wary eye on the two paramedics holding down the irrational, grieving Jake.

When he had cleared the tops of the trees and the power lines, Reese took a deep breath and let it out slowly. That was close. For a few minutes there, he'd wondered if they'd make it without mishap. He knew just how poor Jake must've felt, watching helplessly as Samantha and Andrew whisked away the woman he loved. Still, the way Jacob plowed into Samantha ticked him off. Thank goodness she wasn't hurt.

As he banked around toward Trinity, Reese became aware of problems in the back with their patient

"Andrew, get me two more units of blood. We're losing her pressure." Samantha's voice came through his headset. "Come on, where is she bleeding?"

"Her rhythm is fine," Andrew commented. "I think if she was bleeding internally, she'd be more tacky."

"Not if she has cardiac tamponade or a hemothorax," Samantha responded. "My instincts tell me it's her heart, but I can't listen to her heart tones and lung sounds to know for sure."

"Do you need me to find a place to land?" Reese asked, revealing he was flying and listening to the conversation at the same time. With helmets on and communication through an intercom, he understood the limitations of air transport. At least he could get them to Trinity or an alternate location, quickly. "I don't mind, whatever is best for the patient."

"No, thanks, Reese. I'm going to place a cardiac needle to relieve the pressure. Just get us to Trinity as fast as you can, okay?"

"Roger." Thank heavens, this was a short trip. They were only five to seven minutes from their destination, so there wasn't much he could do except climb a few more feet in altitude in an effort to use the tailwind to its greatest advantage.

"Wow!" Andrew's voice came through the helmet loudly. "Look at all that blood!"

"Reese, please radio the base to request that a cardiothoracic surgeon be on standby," Samantha said. "I think Becky is going to need open heart surgery related to chest trauma."

"Roger that." Reese quickly flipped the switch to get in contact with the base, rattling off Samantha's instructions.

The paramedic base responded to his call, and he gauged the time remaining until they reached Trinity Medical Center. "ETA three minutes," he informed them.

"Thank goodness," Andrew muttered.

"Look, her blood pressure is improving. We're doing all right. Just keep giving her more blood while I hold the needle steady," Samantha ordered.

"You got it."

Reese listened intently as he approached Trinity's helipad. He radioed the base to inform them he was about to land. Within moments, he set the chopper down in the center of the helipad.

"All clear," he informed them.

Samantha didn't waste any time. He watched as she and Andrew unloaded their patient and wheeled her quickly to the waiting elevators.

There was nothing more he could do. Reese sat back in his seat and rubbed a hand over his eyes. This was why he had needed to fight his secret desire to spend time alone with Samantha. How would he ever survive another loss like the one he experienced with Valerie?

Very simply, he wouldn't.

Poor Jake. Reese could only hope that Samantha's quick diagnosis had saved Becky's life. But as he waited for Samantha to return, he realized telling himself to keep away from Samantha was the easy part. The hard part would be listening to the logical voice in his head.

Because every instinct he possessed screamed at him to grab Samantha and to hang on tight.

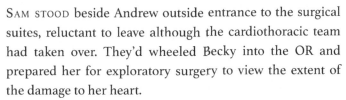

SAM STOOD beside Andrew outside entrance to the surgical suites, reluctant to leave although the cardiothoracic team had taken over. They'd wheeled Becky into the OR and prepared her for exploratory surgery to view the extent of the damage to her heart.

"Hey, she'll be fine." Andrew touched her lightly on the arm. "Come on, we better go."

She nodded and followed Andrew back to the elevator, riding up to the rooftop landing pad where Reese waited in the Lifeline chopper.

There hadn't been time to dwell on the incident at the scene while in flight, as her patient's condition had been too critical. But now the entire event seemed surreal. Never before had she been nearly attacked by a distraught family member at a crash scene. If not for Reese holding the guy back, they wouldn't have gotten out of there in time to get Becky safely transported to Trinity.

Outside, Andrew signaled to Reese who gestured for them to climb inside the helicopter. Andrew began putting supplies away, cleaning up the bloodstains with a bleach wipe.

Sam helped, listening intently as Reese communicated with the base about to take off. His deep voice was mesmerizing. She could listen to him all day, every day.

The trip to Lifeline would be quick, she knew, unless they received another call. Reese's husky voice was calm. He'd been cool and steady even while holding back Jake.

What would it take to ruffle his feathers? Sam wasn't sure she wanted to find out.

Back inside Lifeline's lounge, Andrew made a beeline for

the coffee machine. Sam hung back, waiting for Reese, following him into the debriefing room.

"I need to thank you for what you did back there." She touched his arm lightly, but the heat of his skin radiating through the long sleeve of his flight suit had her drawing back quickly. She hoped he didn't notice her irrational response. "For a minute, I thought our buddy Jake was going to grab her and take off running."

Reese shook his head. "Yeah, I was worried for a few minutes myself, more so that he'd try to jump on while we were taking off." He looked at her intently, and his voice dropped intimately. "I wanted to punch him when he knocked you aside like that."

She hoped her blush wasn't too obvious. "I'm fine. He wasn't trying to hurt me."

"I know." Reese scrubbed his hands over his face. "But he almost did. I get he wanted to ride along, but can you imagine what would've happened if he'd gotten into the helicopter with us?"

"I don't even want to think about it," Sam admitted, suppressing a shiver. Remembering how she'd had to draw blood from the area around Becky's heart, she felt certain he would have interfered with her ability to save Becky's life. "I thought he was going off the deep end."

"He still may, if she doesn't make it." Reese's voice was quiet as he dropped into a chair and stared down at his feet. "I hope she does."

Sam tilted her head, a puzzled frown on her brow. Reese appeared really troubled by this recent air rescue, and she sensed there was something more going on in his head. His thick brown hair made her want to run her fingers through the strands in an attempt to ease his discomfort. Instead, despite knowing she couldn't get close, she leaned forward.

"Hey," she said softly. "Are you all right?"

"Me?" He raised his gaze to hers, his expression guarded. "Why wouldn't I be?"

The wounded expression had vanished, making Sam wonder if she'd imagined it. Still, she continued to press. "I don't know. You seem—sad."

"No. I'm fine." He turned in his seat to stare at the satellite monitor as if the screen held the answers to world peace. Was this all an attempt to avoid her gaze? He could ask her questions about her personal life, but she couldn't ask anything about his?

She was disappointed by the thought.

"There's a storm warning for tomorrow."

"Hmm." Obviously, he didn't want to talk to her. For the first time, she realized Reese possessed secrets of his own. Secrets he wasn't willing to share.

And for some strange reason, she grew more determined to find out exactly what those secrets were.

5

Andrew popped his head into the debriefing room. "Hey, I gotta head over to Trinity for our post-flight follow-up visits."

As much as Sam really wished for a window to peer into Reese's mind to understand what he was thinking, the idea of post-flight visits distracted her. "Could I do them? I'd really like to see how some of our patients are faring."

The paramedic hesitated. "There's no reason you couldn't, except the visits are part of my job, not yours. You're the doctor."

Samantha didn't care whose job they were. Turning over the care of her patients was the hardest part of being a flight physician, and she often wondered how her patients were doing long after she left them. "I don't mind, honestly. Kate showed me how to fill out the paperwork during training."

Andrew shrugged and handed over the clipboard. "Go ahead, then, if you want to."

"Thanks." Sam glanced at the list of names. Jamie's was at the top of the list. There were at least three other patients in addition to Jamie that needed to be checked on. She glanced at Reese. "Do you want to come along?"

He hesitated, then shook his head. "I think there's some rule against giving pilots confidential medical information unless it's directly related to the flight. Go on, I'll wait here and watch Mitch check over the helicopter."

She should have realized this wasn't something the pilot could do. The Federal privacy rules were strict, but in her mind, Reese was so much more than a simple chopper pilot. "Okay. I'll be back soon," she promised.

"Just hurry back if a call comes in," Reese cautioned.

"I will." Sam flashed a quick smile, then grabbed her bulky Lifeline jacket and headed outside.

The trip to Trinity was short as the Lifeline hangar was strategically located nearby. While she walked, her thoughts dwelled on Reese. She really enjoyed flying with him; he was incredibly easy to work with. Of all the pilots, he was the most in tune with what was going on with the patient during transport.

Had she imagined that hint of sorrow in his eyes? She knew he wasn't married, she'd heard the other female residents and the flight nurses talking about Reese in the early days of her training. He was always polite, but she noticed he didn't flirt with the female staff.

Because he wasn't interested? Last night, when he'd walked her to her apartment door, the heated awareness between them had been a palpable thing. She couldn't have imagined the moment she thought he might kiss her. If anything, she knew better than anyone how not wanting to be interested was very different than actual indifference. After all, her emotions had a way of reacting without her permission.

Especially when it came to Reese.

At the information desk in the lobby of Trinity Medical Center, she asked for the room numbers of the patients she needed to see. Jamie was in the medical intensive care unit, so she decided to stop there first.

She found Jamie's bedside without difficulty. Sam entered the room, then belatedly realized a male visitor was seated next to the patient's bed.

"Oh, I'm sorry for intruding," she apologized quickly. "I didn't see you there. My name is Dr. Samantha Kearn. I was the flight physician who helped transport Jamie down from Cedar Ridge."

The man bent to press a kiss to Jamie's forehead, then stood and extended his hand to greet her. "Pleased to meet you. I'm George, Jamie's husband. I want to thank you for bringing her to Trinity. Although she's still very sick, the doctors here have been great. I think she's finally starting to show signs of improvement."

"I'm glad to hear it." Samantha shook his hand, then peeked up at the monitor overhead where the patient's vital signs were prominently displayed. She was grateful to note that Jamie was indeed more stable. The patient's husband remained standing, but he reached out and took his wife's limp hand in his. Sam was touched by the pure devotion in George's gaze as it rested on his critically ill wife.

"So, how are you holding up?" she asked him. The poor guy appeared exhausted. "You need to take care of yourself too, you know. You won't do your wife any good by getting sick yourself."

George's smile was lopsided. "You sound just like the nurses around here. They're always telling me to get more rest." His expression clouded as he gazed at his wife. "I don't think I'll be able to rest until Jamie is home with me where she belongs."

Samantha blinked back empathetic tears. For a moment, the sorrow in his eyes reminded her of the fleeting expression on Reese's face earlier. Poor Jamie and poor George. Their love was obviously strong. She hoped for both of their sakes that Jamie would get better soon. "I understand. I'll come back and check in on her again in a few days."

Jamie's husband nodded, and Samantha turned to leave. Next to Jamie's name on the clipboard in hand she wrote, "Critical but stable."

As she walked to the trauma ICU on the third floor, Samantha thought about her own marriage. She couldn't imagine Dennis being so supportive. But she could see Reese acting very much like George had, completely devoted to his wife.

A woman would be lucky to be loved like that.

She shook off the flash of self-pity and glanced down at her clipboard. What was she thinking, to be jealous of a critically ill patient? So what if Dennis hadn't loved her? She had her health and her career. What more did she want? She needed to count her blessings.

In the trauma ICU, Sam was happy to discover how the patient who'd suffered a work-related injury, which had nearly amputated his arm, was doing well after thirty-one hours of surgery to reattach the limb. When she walked in, she found the trauma ICU nurses packing up his supplies to move him to a regular room.

She spent a few minutes chatting with the grateful patient. She hadn't transported him, but he remembered bits and pieces of the flight and wanted her to thank everyone who had taken care of him. She promised she would.

The last two patients on her list were already in general rooms, ready to be discharged within a few days. She jotted her notations alongside their names on the clipboard and repressed the urge to go upstairs to visit Jamie again. As a physician, Jamie's complicated medical course intrigued her. Sam had chosen emergency medicine for the variety, but at times like this, she wondered if critical care wouldn't have been a better option. She wanted to do an in-depth chart review on Jamie's case to see if there was anything they may have missed. Not that she didn't trust the critical care team, because she did. Still, she liked taking all the signs and symptoms patients presented with and putting the puzzle pieces together until they fit into a diagnosis.

Samantha comforted herself with the knowledge that Jamie was getting the best care possible. There wasn't anything more she could do for her now.

Taking the stairs to the lobby level, she headed toward the front door. Her footsteps slowed when she saw a tall blond-haired man standing off in the corner, talking on his cell phone. She could only see a part of his profile, but it was enough that she sucked in a quick breath and strained to get a better look at his face. At that moment he turned, and her heart dipped when she recognized him.

Dennis. What on earth was he doing here? Sweat dampened her arms beneath her turtleneck sweater, and she instinctively ducked behind a tall rubber tree plant, hiding from view.

Her hands began to tremble, and she clasped them tightly together. Why was her ex-husband here at Trinity? Was he following her? Even if he was, did it matter? She didn't have anything to say to him.

No matter how hard he pleaded, she wasn't ever going back.

Her eyes widened when she saw Dennis turn and shake hands with the gray-haired physician wearing a white lab coat. She recognized Dr. Ben Harris, her boss. Why on earth would her ex-husband be meeting with the medical director of the emergency department? Dennis was a pharmaceutical sales representative, but Milwaukee wasn't part of his territory. Or at least it hadn't been while they'd been married. At the time, Dennis had been based in Chicago.

Things could have changed since their separation and subsequent divorce.

Her pager went off, and she read the display describing a request for an ICU to ICU transfer. Samantha didn't want to see Dennis, or talk to him, but duty won out over the desire to hide. Keeping her gaze averted, she pulled up the edges of her Lifeline jacket to hide her face and quickly wove through the crowd to the front doors. With every step, she expected to hear Dennis call out to her.

But he didn't.

Outside she quickened her pace until she was running back to Lifeline as if the devil himself was nipping at her heels. Reese and Andrew were waiting impatiently.

"Ready to go?" Reese asked.

"Yes." Struggling to catch her breath, she tossed aside the clipboard and climbed into the helicopter, with Andrew close on her heels.

Once they had their helmets on and were connected to the communication system, Andrew tapped her knee to get her attention.

"How did the post-flight visits go?" he asked.

"Great. They went fine." She forced herself to smile, reminding herself Dennis was a part of her past not her future. He was a pharmaceutical sales rep, and for all she knew, Trinity Medical Center was part of his new territory. She didn't like it, but she knew she had no choice but to get over it.

Sam waited for Reese to finish communicating with the paramedic base to find out their destination. "So, tell me about this transport."

"Our patient is a thirty-three-year-old male who'd been snowmobiling near Two Rivers when he crashed into a tree. He lives here in Milwaukee, and his family has requested he be transferred to Trinity Medical Center. Apparently, he has multiple fractures and will need extensive surgery and rehab, which they can't supply up there."

"He's stable, then?"

Andrew shrugged. "Relatively speaking. He's suffered a serious head injury, and apparently, he's a smoker, so his lungs aren't in the greatest shape. It will make it more difficult to get him weaned off the ventilator."

Samantha nodded in understanding. "Reese? How long is the flight to Two Rivers?"

"At least an hour and a half." His deep voice rumbled through her headset. "Settle in for a long ride."

A flash of disappointment speared her heart. She normally didn't mind long flights, but in this case, she'd have preferred to sit up front with Reese.

Settling back against the seat, she stared outside. Their route took them over Lake Michigan. Two Rivers was located close to the lakeshore, and there was nothing but water for as far as she could see beneath them.

Twenty minutes into their ninety-minute flight, Samantha realized the air was full of snow. She leaned forward, peering out the window.

"Reese, what's with all the snow?" she asked.

"Lake effect. When the cold air meets the warmer water, the result is wet snow. I'm heading farther inland to avoid the worst of it. We should be fine."

Samantha tried to relax, but she couldn't help remembering how it had been weather like this that had caused the ice to form on the chopper blades. She trusted Reese implicitly and reminded herself that worrying was useless.

An abrupt dip of the helicopter had her clutching the armrests for support.

"Everyone all right back there?" Reese's warm husky voice immediately came through her headset.

"We're fine." Samantha glanced out the window to see thick flakes. "More lake effect snow?"

"Yes, it's getting worse, and the wind has kicked up dramatically. If we can't escape the brunt of the storm by flying inland, we may have to abort." Reese's tone was grim.

Oh boy. Samantha drew in a deep breath. Never had she been in a situation where they'd had to abort a flight, but the erratic up-and-down movements of the helicopter were such that she wasn't about to complain. Thankfully, she didn't get airsick—at least, not that she knew of. This wasn't exactly the time she wanted to test the theory, though, either. "Roger. Let us know if there's something we need to do."

"Nothing right now. Just hang tight."

Yeah, she was hanging tight. Sam tried to comfort herself with the knowledge that their patient was stable at Two Rivers, and if they didn't get there to pick him up today, there was always the chance they could try again the next morning when the weather settled down.

Peering out the window, she couldn't see any sign of the lake or, for that matter, the shoreline. How on earth was Reese flying? Between the wind and the snow, she couldn't imagine this was any better than flying in fog.

Reese communicated with the base while she and Andrew listened. Finally, after what seemed like an hour, but in reality was probably only another ten minutes, Reese made the decision to turn back.

"Base, we need to abort this flight. Visibility has dropped to below ten feet. I can't proceed safely with the wind gusts tossing us around up here like a kite."

"Roger, Lifeline, will notify the hospital in Two Rivers. They can either arrange for ground transport or we can try again in the morning."

"Ten-four."

Sam could tell Reese didn't like calling a halt to the transport, but looking outside, she couldn't blame him for the decision. Especially considering the wind. The safety straps of her harness dug into her shoulders, and the helicopter dipped roughly again.

As much as she wanted to be able to help the patient who still needed to be transported, Sam couldn't deny she would be very glad to get both of her feet back on stable ground. If they manage to land in one piece, she was going to give Reese a big hug.

REESE'S HANDS were slick with sweat around the stick as he finally landed the helicopter on the Lifeline helipad. For a moment, he closed his eyes in relief, sending up a silent prayer of thanks. They'd made it. There had been several moments where he'd had his doubts. The storm he'd read about wasn't due until tomorrow night, but the weather over the Great Lakes was always dicey. The lake effect snow along with the high winds had been a double whammy.

He shut down the chopper, then climbed out, doing his best to ignore his wobbly knees. Samantha and Andrew were already standing there, waiting for him. He pulled off his helmet, prepared for the brunt of Samantha's wrath, when she suddenly threw her arms around his shoulders and hugged him tight.

Stunned, he didn't react quickly enough to hug her back before she stepped away. "What was that for?"

Her smile was bright and maybe a little brittle. "For getting us back safely."

The surge of protectiveness caught him unawares. Having his life in danger was bad enough, but risking Samantha's life was inconceivable. He swallowed hard and wished his hands would stop shaking.

Their shift was nearly over. Reese verified with the base that they were only in red flying conditions for calls around the lakeshore. Inland calls were still a viable option.

As they split up to file the respective reports, Reese wished for time alone with Samantha to see how she was doing. The turbulent flight must have bothered her more than she'd admitted for her to hug him like that. He couldn't afford to think of her spontaneous gesture as anything more than relief.

Yet, he really wished he'd returned her hug.

His stomach rumbled with hunger as their lunch had been nothing more than a quick sandwich. Was Samantha hungry, too?

He was surprised by the urge to ask her out for dinner. Reese didn't date other Lifeline staff. Didn't date at all, in fact. Over the years since the crash, he'd never wanted to. His heart belonged to Valerie.

Until now. Why the sudden desire to spend more time with Samantha? He could tell himself he only wanted to make sure she was okay, but that would be a lie. Oh, he did care about her state of mind, but that wasn't all. The hug had awakened every nerve ending in his body. He longed to hold her close, to stroke his hand along her back, to bury his hand in her glorious red hair.

To kiss her, to see if she tasted nearly as good as she looked.

After their debriefing to the next shift, Samantha prepared to leave. He quickened his pace to catch up to her, but she beat him to her car.

"Samantha, wait," he called as she opened the driver's door.

She lifted a brow. "What's the matter?"

He tucked his bare hands into the pockets of his jacket, protecting them from the cold. "I thought maybe we could get something to eat. Lunch wasn't much, if you recall. And we're both off work tomorrow." *That's right, keep it simple. Friendly. This doesn't have to be a date.*

"Oh, I don't think so. But thanks for asking." She dipped her head, but he noticed a slight blush tinged her cheeks. "See you later, Reese."

"Sure. Later." For a moment, he stood there and watched as she slid behind the wheel and dutifully put on her seatbelt. Since they both lived in the same apartment complex, he decided to follow her home. He quickly climbed into his truck before she could leave without him.

Only she didn't. When he realized there was something keeping her stationary, he left the warm interior of his truck to brave the cold. He tapped on her window. "What's wrong?"

She reluctantly opened the door. "My car won't start." Frustration laced her tone.

"Battery," he suggested, poking his head inside to look at the dash. He could troubleshoot helicopter engines much easier than car engines. Besides, it was too cold to stand out here for long. "Did you leave a light on? Or forget to close the door all the way?"

"I don't think so. Could be my battery needs to be replaced, though. I think my mechanic mentioned something to that effect last year." Samantha curled her fingers into fists, and he could hear the defeat in her tone. "Guess I'll have to call a tow truck."

"Why don't you let me take you home?" Reese quickly offered. He could jump-start her car, but then it may not work again the next morning. Her car would be safe in the parking lot outside the Lifeline hangar. And yeah, if he were honest, he'd admit he was looking forward to spending more time with her. "We can take care of your car tomorrow. Look on the bright side, at least we don't have to be into work early."

She hesitated in a way that made it clear she wasn't keen on going with him. It hurt to know she didn't trust him enough to give her a lift. Samantha stared out through the windshield for so long he had to stamp his feet to keep his toes from freezing in the chilly air. Maybe he should have simply fetched his jumper cables. Car trouble wasn't the end of the world. This was just a friendly offer to help, and he was about to say so when she finally nodded.

"Sure, I guess you can take me home."

"I promise your car will be okay here. And we'll get a new battery replaced in the morning."

She nodded. "Sounds good."

Since she seemed to be accepting her fate, he couldn't help pushing his luck. "And what about dinner? I mean, we need to eat, right?"

With a wry grin, she eyed him suspiciously. "If I didn't know better, I'd think you sabotaged my car on purpose."

His eyes widened in horror. "I didn't! I would never do something like that."

She smiled at his reaction. "Yeah, I don't think that's your style. All right, dinner, too."

Reese couldn't prevent a huge grin from spreading over his features. Maybe he was a fool, but he hadn't looked forward to spending time with a beautiful woman in what seemed like forever. Ignoring the warning signals bleeping urgently in his brain, he opened her door and offered his hand. She hesitated only for a moment, a motion so slight he would've missed it if he hadn't been so in tune with her every nuance.

Then she placed her ungloved hand in his. He liked the feel of her small, strong, very capable hand. Awed by her trust, he slowly drew her to her feet. In that moment, he knew his fate was sealed.

He could no longer stay away from Samantha any more than he could give up flying.

6

Sam knew she was in trouble when Reese's warm fingers curled firmly around hers. This deliberate touch seemed much different than the impulsive hug she'd bestowed on him earlier. Despite the cold, heat skipped along the nerve endings in her arm. When they were flying together, his voice was a rudder in a turbulent sea. But now his touch heightened the sense of an impending storm. She needed to pull away, to establish some space between them.

Heck, she needed to *breathe*.

His truck was parked right behind her car, so he didn't hold her hand for long. As soon as he'd tucked her into the passenger seat, he slammed the door and jogged around the truck to slide in beside her.

There, much better. Or so she thought, until he turned the key in the ignition and turned toward her. He was close. Much too close. "So, what are you in the mood for?"

You. She bit her tongue to prevent herself from blurting out the ridiculous truth. Food. He'd asked what she wanted to eat.

Nibbling on him wasn't an option.

"Hmm, really, I don't care. Whatever you feel like is fine with me." The way her stomach clenched, she doubted she'd be able to eat anything, no matter what he chose. Despite the fact that he'd played it cool, it still felt like a date.

Except she didn't date. She didn't go out with men at all.

In the dark interior of the truck, she couldn't read his expression. "Chinese takeout?" His voice held a distinct note of hopefulness.

She took pity on him. "Sure, sounds good."

"You like Chinese?" He divided his attention between her and the road.

"Doesn't everyone?" She clasped her hands in her lap to keep them warm. The air vents were still blasting frigid air. She should have worn gloves. Then she wouldn't have had this insane reaction to the touch of his palm against hers.

"Not necessarily," Reese argued softly. "Some women insist on always eating salads. Drives me crazy, as I tend to have an adventurous appetite."

"Really?" Sam wondered if he meant he had an appetite for something other than mere food but chose to ignore the innuendo. "So, what's your favorite Chinese dish?"

"Yu-Hsiang chicken, but a lot of places don't have it. They tend to cater toward the American style of Chinese cuisine. I'm not picky, though. Anything wrapped in an egg roll works for me."

She tilted her head to look at him. She'd gotten the impression he'd been at Lifeline for a while, but she didn't know much about Reese's past or the secrets he may have buried deep beneath the surface. "Have you actually been there? To China?"

"Nah." He flashed a quick, lethal grin. "I just like to eat. I'm the guy who goes to an ethnic restaurant and orders whatever the house specialty is. You'd be amazed at the weird stuff I've eaten. Snake, rabbit..."

"Don't tell me," she joked, raising a hand to make him stop. "I don't want to ruin my appetite."

Reese pulled up at a small Chinese restaurant a few blocks from their apartment complex that she hadn't even known existed. She offered to wait in the car, but he insisted she accompany him inside, encouraging her to help pick out a variety of items. When they had enough white boxes to feed half the population of Beijing, he carried them outside and stashed them in the back seat.

A spicy scent filled the interior of the truck, making her mouth water with anticipation as they drove. Soon the Oak Terrace apartment buildings loomed into view. He paused at the intersection of the complex, glancing at her questioningly. "Your place or mine?"

"Mine." Her breath caught in her throat as he turned into the drive leading to the north building. She wanted to place a hand over her racing heart. Good grief, she needed to get a grip. This was only dinner. She hadn't agreed to anything more.

Although, inviting Reese into the intimacy of her apartment made her wonder what it was like to kiss him. What was wrong with her? She had no idea why her hormones had begun to run amuck.

Reese carried the huge bag holding their dinner as he followed her inside. Sam glanced around the interior of her apartment, reassuring herself that the place was reasonably neat, before opening the door wide to let him in.

"I'll call a friend of mine who owns the garage to see about your car, if you don't mind opening boxes." He set the bag on the table. "If I call him now, it's possible he'll get a chance to work on your car first thing in the morning."

"Of course." Samantha willed her fingers to stop shaking as she pulled several containers out of the bag and began to open them. Surely she could share a meal with a friend without making a big deal out of the situation.

She listened as Reese gave his buddy the details about her car, including the directions to where they'd left the vehicle along with the information about her apartment so he could come and get the keys. She pulled plates, silverware, and glasses out of the cupboard, set them on the table, then glanced around her stark apartment with dismay. What she wouldn't give for a little background music. She toyed with the idea of opening her music app on her phone but then began to stress over what kind of music Reese might like compared to her preference toward country rock.

There she went again, worrying about things that were unimportant. Why did she care what Reese thought of her favorite type of music?

She was letting Dennis mess with her head.

Reese hung up and eyed the spread of steaming white boxes on the table with glee. If he noticed the barren walls and lack of interior decorating of her living space, he didn't comment. "Looks great."

"Dig in," she invited. Her eyes widened as Reese heaped food on his plate, taking a sampling from every single container. He still wore his flight suit from work, and she wondered where on his lean frame he put all the food.

When she spooned sweet-and-sour chicken and broccoli over her rice, her appetite returned with a vengeance.

"I was hungrier than I realized," she admitted a few minutes later, taking a break from her meal.

Reese's brown eyes darkened as his gaze met hers. "I'm glad."

His eyes seemed to hold her captive. Samantha's hand

froze halfway to her mouth, and a big drop of sweet-and-sour sauce plopped onto the table beneath her fork. She swallowed hard and dabbed at the spot with her napkin.

Tension simmered between them. Oh boy, she was in over her head. Way over. The silence was deafening.

Until her doorbell buzzed loudly. She startled so badly her fork clattered to her plate.

If Reese noticed her obvious overreaction, he didn't let on. "Must be Vince." Reese nonchalantly stood as if he hadn't tried to singe her with his heated gaze. He held out his hand. "I need to give him your keys."

"What? Oh, ah, sure." She stood and crossed over to fumble with her purse until she found the keys and handed them over. This needed to stop. She hated feeling like a green medical student at her first autopsy. She was almost a board-certified emergency medical physician. About time she acted like one. She was in control of her life and planned to stay that way.

In a matter of minutes, Reese had given Vince her keys with instructions to call him in the morning with the status of her car. Vince left with a cheerful wave. Sam resisted the urge to call him back.

Reese shut the door behind him and turned to face her. "So, where were we?"

"Eating a friendly dinner." She added emphasis to the word *friendly*.

"Of course." He returned to his seat across from her. "Everything tastes wonderful."

"You say that as if I slaved all day over a hot stove." Sam rolled her eyes and pushed her empty plate away. "Thanks for calling Vince to take care of my car."

"No problem." Reese ate until he'd cleaned every last

speck of rice from his heaping plate. She couldn't remember when she'd enjoyed watching a man eat. Reese might consider himself adventurous, but it was better than what she was used to. Dennis had quirky tastes when it came to food. He would only eat certain things prepared a specific way. And more often than not he'd claimed she'd done it wrong.

Whoa, enough of those thoughts. Sam stood and began to close the boxes that still contained food. "You're going to have to take these leftovers with you. I'll never be able to eat all this."

"Yum, breakfast."

She shook her head with a hint of amusement. "I'm sure there's enough here for your breakfast, lunch, and dinner."

"I bet you're right." He caught her hand as she placed a box in the original bag. "Thank you, Samantha."

She went still, caught off guard by his obvious sincerity. "For what?"

"For sharing dinner with me." His thumb lightly stroked the back of her hand. "I really didn't want to eat alone."

"You're welcome." Sam needed to sit, or she knew she would fall flat on her face. Her physical reaction to Reese was crazy.

He slowly stood, still claiming her hand. When he stepped closer, she sensed his intent and told herself to step back, out of reach.

Her feet didn't listen to her brain's feeble command. As if she were a puppet dangling from a string, she watched him lean toward her. His mouth brushed hers, lightly at first as if testing the water, then when she didn't pull away or protest, he kissed her again.

Deeply. Hungrily. His mouth possessed hers. Heat flared,

hot and needy. She wrapped her arms around his lean waist, savoring the taste of his mouth on hers. His strong arms cradled her close without overwhelming her.

When her head began to spin from lack of oxygen, he slowly ended the kiss, dragging his hands from her shoulders to her arms and then to her hands. She reluctantly stepped back, struggling to breathe.

His voice was low and husky with desire as he stepped away. "I'd better go."

"No," her body screamed in protest. "Yes," her mind insisted.

He'd made it to her door before she stopped him. "Reese."

He swung around to face her. "Yeah?"

"I—don't think I'm ready for relationship." The words came out in a rush, but it was only fair to warn him. As wonderfully nice as he was, this *thing*—whatever it was between them—couldn't go anywhere.

His smile was crooked. "I know. Me either. Except I think it's too late."

"Too late?" What did that mean?

"I don't seem to have a choice where you're concerned."

Her dismay must've shown in her eyes because he quickly smiled. "Hey, there's no need to panic. Just promise me one thing."

"If I can," she hedged. Her fingers curled around one of her kitchen chairs for support. She didn't give promises lightly. Not anymore.

"Promise you'll let me help keep you safe, at least for the next few months until you finish your training at Lifeline." His gaze turned somber. "As a friend, Samantha, if that's what you prefer. Once you graduate from training, I'll let you go."

Madness. What he proposed was sheer madness. She wasn't in any real danger other than some of the routine risks of her job. The last thing her heart needed was to be tangled up with another man. Even more, she couldn't afford to give up her newfound independence. Reese had no idea how much he was asking of her.

"I don't know if I can," she confessed.

He didn't yell or protest, just gave her that same even look. "Okay. Just think about it. I'd never ask for more than you're willing to give." He opened her apartment door. "Good night, Samantha."

She didn't want him to go but forced herself to stay where she was, far too tempted to reach out to the man whose strength drew her as much as the glimmer of sorrow in his eyes. He was long gone before she answered in a quiet voice, "Good night, Reese."

Reese didn't remember much about getting home.

He could still taste Samantha on his lips. Could see the wide, dazed expression in her eyes when he lifted his mouth from hers. With a groan, he stared up at the ceiling of his bedroom, every nerve in his body shimmering with awareness of what he'd held, savored, then lost.

He wanted Samantha. In a way he hadn't wanted a woman in a long time. She wasn't ready for relationship. A rusty laugh strangled in his throat. He could relate to that. But he'd told her the truth. He'd sworn not to get involved, yet here he was, tangled into knots over a tiny redheaded flight physician. Tumbling headfirst into what certainly resembled a relationship, pitfalls and all.

With an effort, he pulled himself away from that line of

thinking. Samantha wasn't ready for a relationship, so he'd honor the terms of his proposition. He really did want to keep her safe, at least while she was flying under his care.

Surely they could remain friends, at least until she'd finished her training.

He must've drifted off to sleep at some point during the wee hours of the morning because when he abruptly opened his eyes, bright light poured through the window of his bedroom.

Blinking, he peered outside. The temperature was probably well below freezing, but the sunlight gave the impression of warmth. A perfect day to spend outside. And on his day off, too. What would Samantha say if he proposed a little outing?

He mentally smacked himself in the head. She only wanted friendship, nothing more. He needed to find something else to occupy his mind.

The ringing of his phone startled him from thoughts of Samantha. Praying there wasn't some sort of problem at Lifeline, he warily picked up the receiver. "Yeah?"

"Reese?"

"Hey, Vince." He relaxed at the sound of his buddy's voice and padded to the kitchen. "What's up? Don't tell me you've already looked at Samantha's car?"

"As a matter of fact, I did."

"Was it the battery? She thought it might need to be replaced." Reese tucked the phone between his shoulder and his ear so he could dig the leftover Chinese food out of the fridge. He never minded eating leftovers, although they would've tasted far better if Samantha were here to share them.

"Sort of."

Reese frowned as he opened the containers. Vince's tone was weird, evasive. "What do you mean, sort of? Samantha's car trouble is either the result of a defunct battery or not."

"The battery is defunct all right. But not by accident."

A shiver of dread slithered down his spine, and he carefully set the container of Chinese on the table. "Someone messed with her battery on purpose? How can you tell?"

"Gee, maybe by the round indentations made by a hammerhead where it smashed the battery? Hard enough to crack the casing. Battery acid has leaked all over the place, creating a big mess."

"A hammer." Reese sank into a chair and tunneled his fingers through his hair. "I bet her ex, Dennis Markowitz, wrecked her battery on purpose."

"My assessment is that this damage was absolutely intentional. What's the deal? Do you know this guy, Markowitz?"

"No." But he'd sure like to. The flower delivery had been annoying but basically harmless. Smashing a battery with a hammer turned the violence up a notch. "Can you fix it?"

"Yeah, shouldn't be too bad. I'll have to replace the battery, of course. Cleaning up the interior where the acid leaked all over will be the hardest part. Can't tell you for sure what parts the acid may have ruined until I dig into the engine."

"Do what you can, Vince." Reese toyed with the carton of Chinese food. His hearty appetite had seemingly vanished. "Send the bill to me."

"Sure, no problem." Vince hesitated. "Do you want me to call Samantha to tell her what happened?"

"No, I'll do it." His stomach clenched at the thought. At least this proved his wanting to keep her safe was more than just an overreaction on his part. It was a necessity. "Just work on getting her car fixed as soon as possible."

"Will do."

"Thanks." Reese hung up the phone. First, he'd shower, then go find Samantha. There wasn't going to be an easy way to soften this blow. Better if he told her in person.

His hair was still damp from the shower when his doorbell buzzed long and loud. Wearing only his jeans and a long-sleeved T-shirt, he crossed to the intercom. "Who is it?"

"Samantha."

"Come on up." Surprised, he pushed the button releasing the lock on the outside door. What had brought Samantha over here? Had she somehow found out the news about her car from Vince?

He opened his apartment door, watching her walk down the hallway toward him. Like him, she was dressed casually in blue jeans. Although she wore a bulky jacket, he could see she wore another of those turtleneck sweaters, this one in bright green.

Why was he developing a weird neck fetish?

"Good morning." He smiled. "Did you walk over from your place?"

"Yes, it's not far." Samantha didn't return his smile—in fact, her pretty brow was furrowed. "I came over to get Vince's phone number. I should have asked for the information last night, before you left."

"Come in." Reese gestured for her to come inside. "I already spoke to Vince."

Her frown deepened. "That's very nice of you, but I'd rather take care of this myself. It's my car."

What was this about? Had something happened to cause

A Doctor's Secret

her change of heart? Reese stood awkwardly in his bare feet. "Are you hungry?" Stalling, he turned back toward the Chinese food he left on the table. "We can eat breakfast."

"No, thanks." Samantha remained where she was, standing near his doorway as if she'd bolt if given half the chance. "If you'd just give me Vince's phone number, I'll be out of your hair."

He didn't think she'd appreciate knowing he liked having her in his hair. And in his apartment. She was so beautiful, but he needed to keep his mind focused on the issue at hand. He noticed her firm stance at his door. With a sigh, he realized she wasn't going to make this easy. "Samantha, I'm sorry to tell you like this, but your car trouble wasn't an accident."

Her wary gaze sharpened. "What do you mean?"

"Sit down. Please," he added when she didn't move.

"Dennis did something to my car, didn't he?" She crossed her arms protectively over her chest.

"Yes." Reese couldn't see the point in lying to her. "He smashed your battery, and it leaked acid all over your engine. I authorized Vince to do the repairs. He's going to get your car fixed as soon as possible."

"You authorized Vince to do the repairs?" Her voice was dangerously soft.

He didn't understand her strange reaction. Why wasn't she more worried about her ex's tendency toward violence? Instead, she seemed annoyed with him. She had been happy enough with his help last night. "Yes. Don't worry, I'll take care of everything."

"No, you won't." Samantha glared at him, fury spiking her stormy gray eyes. Wow, had he ever seen her this angry? "Give me Vince's number. I don't need you taking control, or anyone else for that matter. What part of this don't you understand? It's my car. I want to take care of things myself."

It took a minute for realization to set in. Clearly, her ex-husband had control issues.

And Reese had inadvertently stepped into the mess her ex had left behind.

7

Samantha's entire body vibrated with suppressed fury. Why had she caved under the pressure and accepted help from Reese last night? She should've known better than to rely on a man. Reese was a bulldozer, just like Dennis. One tiny favor and he acted as if he owned her.

Oh, no. Never again.

She straightened her spine, prepared to fight. But instead of arguing, Reese simply went over to his phone, jotted Vince's number on a slip of paper, and crossed the room to hand it to her.

"I'm sorry. You're absolutely right. It's your car. I should have asked Vince to call you first thing this morning."

His quiet apology caught her off guard. Again. Why couldn't he stay true to form? It was easier to resent him when he was being a jerk. And why couldn't he put socks on his feet? She fought to keep her voice steady. "Yes, you should have."

"You're not helpless, Samantha. I know how well you

take care of everything. You literally save lives every day. I just wanted to help. Kind of the way I help by flying you to places where you can do the most good."

The earnest expression in his warm brown eyes made it difficult to hang on to her anger. His damp mink-colored hair curled around his ears. And his bare toes didn't help either. Since when did she notice a man's toes? With a sigh, she took Vince's number and nodded.

"I know." She turned to leave.

"Are you sure you won't stay for breakfast?" His voice stopped her as she opened his door. "I can whip up an omelet if you'd rather have that over Chinese leftovers."

"No, but thanks." She lifted her hand in a simple wave. "See you later."

She thought she heard him say something like, "Count on it," before she closed the door behind her.

Sam lifted her face to the sun as she stepped outside. The warmth after several days of subzero temperatures felt wonderful. The walk from Reese's building to hers wasn't far, and she was proud of the way she didn't glance over her shoulder every ten seconds, looking for Dennis the Menace.

Why had he smashed her car battery? Was this more of his need for control? He'd often used words as weapons, but breaking things was out of character, even for him. What would he break next? She couldn't even begin to guess. Dennis wasn't always ruled by logic.

Even with this new turn of events, she was still royally ticked at herself for having allowed Reese to take over her car problems last night. She should have insisted on standing up for herself. Thoughts of sharing more than a meal with him had obviously clouded her judgment. Well, no more. She would call Vince, making it very clear she was in charge of her car repairs and the bill. Reese was not. He was a nice guy, but if she didn't maintain her independence, what did she have?

Loneliness.

For a moment, her shoulders slumped. How many times over the past year had she wished for someone to lean on? Her family was on the other side of the continent, and keeping close friends during a medical residency wasn't easy. Every month she was shipped off to a new rotation with a whole new group of other residents. At least, that's how the pattern had been until her most recent stint at Lifeline.

Lifeline didn't change residents every month, mostly because of the lengthy flight training. Also, because she'd requested a double rotation. Ben Harris had been more than willing to juggle the schedule in her favor.

Had Dennis really contacted Ben because of her? She shied away from the thought. Dennis probably had a business appointment with Ben. It must be that his sales territory had been changed to include Milwaukee. It was the only logical explanation. There was no reason to think a pharmaceutical sales rep had a special friendship with her boss. Frankly, she didn't envy Dennis's job. As a rule, most of the physicians barely tolerated sales reps. Most of them resented the high cost of pharmaceuticals and didn't hesitate to let the sales reps know of their displeasure.

The fact that Dennis hadn't made it through his residency only worked against him. He hadn't been able to handle the pressure and had dropped out. She knew firsthand how much he resented all physicians for accomplishing something he hadn't been able to do.

Her success had pushed Dennis over the edge. When

she'd excelled in her residency training, she'd noticed his behavior had changed. And not for the better.

With a start, Sam realized she'd arrived at her apartment building. The weather was so nice, she was tempted to keep walking. Too bad she didn't have her car, or she'd consider heading downtown to the lakefront. Wasn't there some sort of Winterfest going on this weekend? How long had it been since she'd done anything for fun?

Too long.

But there was always laundry, and maybe cleaning. Oh joy.

"Samantha."

Heart pounding, she whirled at the sound of her name. Her breath whooshed out of her lungs when she saw Reese standing a few feet behind her, his hands tucked into his coat pockets. "Don't do that to me." Her tone was sharp.

"I'm sorry. I called your name earlier, but you didn't hear me." His dark eyes held regret.

She forced a smile. Her jumpiness wasn't Reese's fault. "I guess I was deep in thought."

He didn't ask what caused her to become lost in her thoughts. Knowing Reese, he'd likely be able to figure it out. Amazingly, Reese knew more about her personal life than anyone.

"Would you be interested in going down to Winterfest with me as one friend to another? We're both off work, and it's such an unusually nice day, it seems a shame to waste it."

How had he read her mind? Sam's first instinct was to refuse, but the alternative of going back to her closed-in, sterile apartment held no appeal. "I have to call Vince," she told him, which wasn't an answer at all.

"I understand. I'll wait."

Still, Sam hesitated. She didn't want to give Reese the wrong impression, but then again, she had made her feelings about relationships very clear. And he'd said friend to friend, so he'd obviously gotten the message. What could it hurt to go down to Winterfest with him? When was the last time she'd had the luxury of going out with a friend?

"All right." She decided quickly before she could analyze things to death and find a reason to talk herself out of it. "Give me a few minutes and I'll be right back."

A hint of a smile flitted across Reese's features. "I'll get my truck and wait for you."

Sam nodded and quickly dashed inside. She called Vince but had to leave a message. Not a big deal since she knew very well Reese had already talked to him. With an unexplained excitement flickering through her veins, she spent a few purely adolescent minutes in front of the mirror, fixing her hair and applying lip gloss. Should she change? No, that would be too noticeable. Calling herself every kind of fool, she grabbed her purse and headed back outside.

When she jumped in the truck beside Reese, he flashed a warm smile. Maybe, with Reese's help, she could forget all about Dennis, at least for a little while.

The lakefront teemed with life, people everywhere walking and jogging. Partially because of the Winterfest activities, including a giant ice sculpture contest taking place right on the shore of Lake Michigan. But more so, she guessed, because of the unseasonably warm weather. Not that temperatures close to forty degrees were exactly warm, but winter in Wisconsin was cold. Like really, really cold. Which made temperatures in the forties more than tolerable.

There was a huge banner announcing a Children's Memorial Hospital fundraiser being held in a few weeks at the lakefront Art Museum. The tickets were expensive, although the money was for a good cause. Too costly for her personal budget, getting rid of Dennis had cleaned out her savings account. Still, she wondered if Lifeline would spring for them. She made a mental note to look into it before she and Reese wandered toward the ice sculpture display.

"Will you look at that?" Reese stopped in front of a guy teetering on a stepladder, intently carving his massive ice sculpture of a hot air balloon. "Very cool."

Sam raised a brow. "Did you always dream of flying, even as a kid?"

Reese didn't take his eyes off the hot air balloon emerging from the block of ice. "Yeah, pretty much. But mostly I was fixated on planes. All sorts of planes. I joined the Air Force straight out of high school just so I could learn to fly planes."

"Planes, huh? So how did you end up flying helicopters?"

He turned toward her and shrugged. "Couldn't afford to be picky. The Air Force needed chopper pilots, so that's the track they sent me. Since I was learning to fly, I wasn't about to complain. And I quickly learned to love the flexibility of the whirlybirds. You can't set a big hulking plane down on a dime."

She could easily imagine Reese in the military. He had a quiet strength that must've helped him endure the tough physical training as well as the constant rules and regulations. She wanted to know more—about his parents, his family, where he grew up. But before she could figure out a non-nosy way to ask, as they wandered amongst the ice sculpture displays, his hand smoothly captured hers.

Distracted by the gesture, the additional questions tumbled right out of her mind. She enjoyed the protective feeling of his hand around hers and knew she should consider pulling away. Wasn't hand-holding a violation of the friendship agreement? His hand was nice, warm and firm without being too tight around hers.

For the life of her, she couldn't bear to give up the slight contact.

He'd promised not to ask for more than she was willing to give, and she couldn't help but believe Reese was the type of guy who kept his promises.

"What about this one?" she asked, pausing in front of a giant ice beetle. "What makes someone want to carve a bug?"

"I don't know, but I like the race car over there." Reese gestured with his hand to the sculpture up ahead. "It's true to scale. I feel like I could jump inside and take a spin."

"Men and their toys," she teased.

"How about an early lunch?" Reese asked after they'd seen each and every ice sculpture. He gestured as they came up alongside a couple of fast-food vendors. "I bet you didn't eat breakfast either."

She hadn't and knew her refusal to stay and eat with him had probably caused him to miss his breakfast, too, since he hadn't wasted any time in following her. "Sure, but I don't want to wait in line. I'd like to sit and look out over the water for a bit."

"Tell me what you'd like, and I'll bring it over," Reese promised.

She made her selection—hot, spicy, Cajun chicken—and handed him a ten. He looked as if he'd argue but reluctantly took the cash. She ambled toward the lakeshore. The rhythmic sound of the waves crashing over the rocks was almost as soothing as Reese's voice flowing through her headset in flight.

Squealing tires, followed by a loud thump-thump, made her turn with a frown. Screams split the air.

"Oh no, he's hit. He's hit!"

Before the woman's screams fully registered, Samantha was running toward the group huddled by the side of the road. She quickly shoved her way through the crowd.

"I'm a doctor. Let me through."

Like a parting of the sea, people moved out of her way. She instantly saw the victim, a man who appeared to be in his late twenties or early thirties dressed in jogging clothes, sprawled along the side of the road. Blood trickled from a wound on his temple, and the odd angle of his legs had her suspecting a pelvic fracture at the very least.

"Someone call nine-one-one," she directed in a stern voice as she knelt at the victim's side.

"I did." Reese materialized by her side. "Do you need help?"

"Not yet." Samantha positioned the man's head to open his airway. He wasn't breathing. Before she could pull a small resuscitation mask from her purse, Reese handed her one.

"Here, I carry one at all times."

Grateful, she took the mask and used it to give the victim rescue breaths. Then, following the ABCs just like they did in the ER, she checked for a pulse.

"No pulse," she muttered before placing her hands over the sternum to perform chest compressions.

"I'll breathe for you." Reese positioned himself at the patient's head.

Good thing the pilots at Lifeline were trained in CPR. Samantha concentrated on performing good chest compressions, counting out loud so Reese would know when to give a breath. They worked together in tandem as if they'd done this hundreds of times before.

"Pulse check," Samantha suggested. "First with compressions." This was a tactic she'd learned in medical school: when you could feel the pulse with chest compressions, it is easier to then stop the compressions to see if there was a spontaneous return of the victim's pulse.

"Pulse good with compressions," Reese informed her.

"Okay. What about now?" She halted her compressions, waiting while he kept his hand in the same place along the carotid artery. She waited a moment, knowing how easy it was to miss a pulse on a victim when your own was pumping in double time.

"No pulse. Continue CPR."

Samantha nodded and began the chest compression routine all over again.

She and Reese performed several rounds of CPR before she heard the distinct wail of sirens. She wished for a chance to do a neuro exam on the patient, but if they didn't maintain his oxygenation with the breathing and chest compressions, there wouldn't be a neuro status to worry about.

The paramedics arrived on scene and quickly took over the rescue breathing with an oxygen tank and Ambu bag. Samantha didn't let up on her chest compressions as they made the switch.

"Are you all right there for a while longer?" one of the paramedics wanted to know.

She nodded. "I'm an emergency medicine resident working at Lifeline."

The paramedic nodded, trusting her skills. Once they had the patient connected to the portable monitoring equipment, she stopped compressions so they could see the underlying rhythm. Seeing V-fib on the monitor, they shocked him. Once, twice, then a third time.

When those shocks didn't convert him, one paramedic quickly placed a breathing tube while the other cut away the man's pants from his thigh. Then he took a gun-like machine out of his bag and placed the tip firmly against the femur bone. He pulled the trigger, sending a needle directly into the center of the patient's bone. While it looked barbaric, Sam knew that injecting medication via the intraosseous needle and into the bone was the quickest way to get medication into the patient's system. They worked over him for another ten minutes, giving more meds and shocking again.

"He's converted into sinus rhythm," one paramedic noted. "Let's get him into the bus."

The paramedics didn't waste a second but picked him up, plunked him onto a gurney and whisked him off, presumably to Trinity Medical Center. Samantha stood there, watching them drive away, feeling at a loss. Normally she would be on the receiving end of getting this patient from the field. Being the first responder on the scene felt extremely odd.

"You're amazing." Reese came up behind her and gently squeezed her shoulders. "You saved his life."

"We saved his life," she corrected, slanting him a look over her shoulder. The need to lose herself in Reese's arms was strong, but she told herself not to be a wimp. "Thanks for your help. I really hope he makes it. At least he has youth on his side."

"If he doesn't make it, it's not because we didn't do our best," Reese observed quietly. He slowly turned her so she was facing him. He reached up to tuck a strand of her hair behind her ear.

"I know." She tried to smile. But the intense expression in Reese's dark eyes practically sent her heart into V-tach. Before she could think of protesting, he pulled her close.

"Samantha." He didn't try to kiss her but tucked her head into the hollow of his shoulder. "This time I think we both need a hug."

She closed her eyes and inhaled the comforting scent of his spicy aftershave. He held her close, but not so hard that she felt as if she were suffocating. His chest was firm, muscular and yet oh so soft.

"Excuse me," the strange voice interrupted them. "I need to ask you a few questions."

Sam raised her head to find a Milwaukee police officer standing beside them. "Of course," she responded.

Reese prevented her from breaking completely free of his embrace, tucking an arm over her shoulder so they could face the officer together.

"What can we do for you?" Sam asked.

"Did you see the car that hit him?"

Samantha slowly shook her head. "No, but I heard the screech of the tires and the double thumps as he was hit."

"That's what I was afraid of." The cop glanced back over his shoulder at the road as if seeking answers there. "Only one woman saw a green car slam on the brakes and hit the jogger, but she didn't get the make of the car or the number off the plates."

From moment, Sam didn't understand. "You mean, this was a hit-and-run?"

The officer's expression was grim. "Yes, and we don't have a clue to point us in the direction of the assailant."

Samantha shivered despite the warmth of Reese's arm

around her shoulders. It was creepy to think that this man had been hit by a driver who had decided to flee the scene. It was one thing to know violence existed, she'd seen more than her fair share, but this struck a little too close to home.

She hoped and prayed that whoever had done this would turn themselves in.

8

Reese frowned and swept a glance around the area. "Someone must have seen something."

"I hope so." The cop's tone did not sound overly optimistic. "If you remember anything, let me know." He moved on to question the next person.

The cheerful, carefree atmosphere at the lakefront turned somber. Several strangers came up to express gratitude for the way they'd worked so hard to save the victim's life. Reese finally drew Samantha away from the crowd, sensing her impatience with the attention.

"I was just doing my job," she muttered under her breath. "You would think these people would understand that."

"You were awesome," Reese corrected softly. "And most of your average everyday citizens don't see that kind of heroism in action except on television."

"I guess." She didn't sound satisfied.

"Still hungry?" Reese doubted it, but his own stomach was rumbling like mad. When he'd heard the brakes squeal and the resounding thump, he'd left the food line to rush over and help. "I really gotta get something to eat."

"Sure, we can order lunch." Her tone lacked enthusiasm. This time, she stood in line beside him. They took their meal over to a large boulder overlooking the lake. The rippling blue water shimmered beneath the sun.

He noticed Samantha didn't do more than pick at her Cajun chicken, but he figured a little nourishment was better than nothing. His appetite was indestructible, enabling him to devour his burger quickly.

The wind picked up, putting a definite chill in the air. He convinced her to walk through the rest of the ice sculpture displays, but even when the hot air balloon won first place, he could tell her heart wasn't into celebrating.

Reese couldn't blame her. He'd been impressed with her calm professionalism during their rescue efforts. She was the one in need of protecting, yet she willingly saved lives every day. Logically he knew her ex couldn't have had anything to do with the hit-and-run accident, especially since the jogger hadn't been anywhere near Samantha when he'd been hit. But the image of the guy bleeding in the street, his leg obviously broken, wouldn't leave him alone. He didn't want to think of what might happen if her ex turned his violence toward her.

"I think I'm ready to head home." Samantha shivered and buried her face in the warmth of her coat. "The wind off the lake has gotten really chilly. The temperature feels as if it's dropped twenty degrees."

"Yeah, I know." He glanced at his watch, then steered them in the direction of where he parked his truck. It wasn't late, not yet five in the afternoon. "But it's still early enough to get in touch with Vince. We might be able to pick up your car on the way home." He couldn't forget how annoyed she was with him earlier that morning. "If you were planning to pick it up today, that is," he hastily added. "If not, that's okay, too."

"Yes, actually I was hoping to pick it up today." She arched a brow at him. "I suppose you just happen to know exactly where Vince's garage is, too, right?"

"Yeah." He sent a cautious glance in her direction as he unlocked the truck. He felt as if you were walking through a minefield. With Samantha, he was quickly beginning to realize that offering to help resembled a cardinal sin. "Why, does that make you mad?"

"No." She blew out her breath in exasperation. "I guess not. I left him a message this morning, but he hasn't gotten back to me. I have his number in my phone so give me a minute to make the call."

Reese listened to her one-sided conversation and was glad when it sounded as if Vince did indeed have her car running again.

"So we're heading to Vince's auto shop?" he asked when she'd disconnected from the call.

"Sure." She stared out the windshield with a frown. "What's with all the traffic?"

"The Bucks are playing at home tonight." Something he should've thought of; they could have avoided much of the traffic by leaving a little earlier. He slanted her a glance. "Not much of a basketball fan?" he guessed.

She shrugged. "I don't really have a lot of time for sports. Probably won't until after I pass my boards."

Over the past year at Lifeline, he'd learned the senior emergency medicine residents were scheduled to take their medical boards in June. It was only February now. "You've already started studying?"

"Well, they're not something you can cram for." Her dry humor made him smile.

"I guess not. I'm amazed you can concentrate at all with everything that's going on in your personal life." These issues with her ex had to be weighing on her shoulders. Didn't her ex know this was an important time for her? Or did he just not care?

"I'm used to it." She looked away, and he instinctively knew the subject was closed. Maybe she was used to it, but she shouldn't have to be. Reese wished, more than anything, he could get Markowitz alone, just for a couple of minutes.

The traffic jam broke up after a few miles. He headed straight for Vince's garage. Although it was difficult, he remained in the truck while she spoke with Vince, watching as they both poked their heads under the hood while Vince pointed out the items he'd fixed or replaced.

Reese wanted to see the damage to battery for himself. But if he got out and demanded Vince show him, Samantha would get upset that he was poking his nose into her business. Besides, after the earlier hit-and-run accident, he figured she didn't need further reminders of violence.

She paid Vince, which frankly grated on his nerves, because he sensed she didn't have cash to spare, then waved at Reese as she climbed into her car. He didn't want the evening to end. His problem, of course, he acknowledged as he followed her home. When he pulled up and parked next to her, she shot him an exasperated glance. But that didn't stop him from getting out of the car to meet up with her.

"You're off duty now, Reese." She slammed her car door with a little too much force. "I don't need a babysitter."

Reese shook his head. "I'm not volunteering for babysitting duty. Please, Samantha, I just want to walk you to your door." And follow her inside. But he kept that thought to himself.

"What, no offer of dinner?" She crossed her arms over her chest. "I'm shocked."

Since he had, in fact, been about to offer to order something in for dinner, he clamped his jaw shut. After a moment he said, "I just don't understand how anyone can forget to eat."

"I don't forget, I just don't have your metabolism," she pointed out as she dug for her key. "Thanks for taking me to Winterfest." She flashed a wry smile. "It certainly was an adventure."

He wasn't blind; the expression on her pretty face clearly indicated she wanted him to leave. Yet he had no intention of following her wishes. "All the way in, Samantha."

For a moment he wondered if he'd pushed a little too hard. Safety wasn't anything to take lightly. He knew only too well what carelessness could bring. Man, the woman could be stubborn when she wanted to be.

"Fine, come on in, then." Annoyed, she used her key to open the apartment door. "Anyone ever tell you you're persistent?"

"Me? Like you should talk." He held the door, then followed her inside. "What's the harm of me walking you in? I'm not about to jump your bones, although they are very lovely bones."

Shocked, she gaped at him. "I never said you would."

He kept his eyes wide, innocent. "Then what's the problem?"

"You're the problem." Samantha used her key to unlock the door of her apartment and, much like the last time, she opened it wide so he could look inside. "See, everything is fine. Good night, Reese."

"What's that?" A white slip of paper caught his eye, partially hidden behind the door. He bent over, pulled it out, then straightened. Words were printed in large block letters. *Come home, or you're next.*

"Oh no. Dennis." Samantha paled, and Reese figured the only thing keeping her upright was the door at her back.

A red haze of anger blurred his vision. He blocked the fury with an effort. "This is an outright threat. You're not staying here. I'm taking you to my place."

"Forget it. I'm not leaving." She looked like she might faint, but her tone was steady.

Incredulous, he stared at her. "You can't be serious. Read this. Do you know what it means? You're next? Next for what, Samantha? Another hit-and-run accident?"

There was a long silence as his words sank deep. Her eyes widened in horror. "He was at the lakefront today, wasn't he? He must've seen the accident. He saw us together." Samantha's voice was hoarse.

Gentling his tone, he agreed. "Yes, so that's why you need to come to my place with me. Do you want to pack a bag?"

"No, Reese." Samantha was so pale her gray eyes looked like dark storm clouds in a sea of white. "I appreciate what you're trying to do, but he's not chasing me out of my home."

"Then I'm not leaving." He followed her inside the apartment, closing the door behind him.

"You're not staying."

He knew she'd argue. It seemed to be her favorite pastime. But he wasn't budging an inch. "I am staying at least until you've reported this to the police."

Relief flooded him when she seemingly ignored him but pulled out her phone to make the call. Reese scrubbed a hand along his jaw as Samantha spoke to the dispatcher. He hadn't wanted the evening to end. But extending the time he could spend with her because of something like this wasn't what he wanted either.

Safety, at least for Samantha, seemed more elusive than ever.

~

SAM WAS FREEZING. She wore a turtleneck sweater and the thermostat in her apartment was cranked to seventy-four degrees, but she was still cold.

She didn't want to believe Dennis had followed her down to the lakefront. Why hadn't she felt his presence? A shiver rippled through her. Maybe she hadn't noticed because of Reese, but the notion didn't make her feel any better. Dennis had been jealously possessive without the least bit of provocation on her part. They were divorced, but she could only imagine what had gone through his mind when he'd seen Reese walking beside her, holding her hand.

The dispatcher claimed two officers were on their way, but Samantha didn't hold out much hope of the investigation actually showing some level of proof that Dennis was behind the note. Knowing Reese was probably hungry again, she offered to throw something together for dinner.

"Why don't I just order out for pizza?" he suggested.

"Sure." She lifted her shoulder. It didn't matter what he ordered, food wasn't high on her list of priorities at the moment.

The pizza arrived before the police did. Reese was annoyed with the fact, but Sam understood. Unfortunately, this was how the system worked. The threat wasn't immediate. There was no need to rush.

When the officer arrived, she gestured to the note. Reese had picked it up, but she refused to touch it. She gave a brief description of how she and Reese had come home from Winterfest to find the note that had been apparently shoved beneath her apartment door.

"What time did you leave this morning?" the officer wanted to know.

She had no idea. With a raised brow, she glanced at Reese. "Close to nine thirty," he responded.

The officer wanted to hear everything that had transpired throughout the day. Samantha condensed the events the best she could and explained about the restraining order. When the officer questioned her about the previous threats, Reese lost his temper.

"You should already know about the previous threats! Didn't she just tell you about the restraining order? How many threats before you take this seriously? It's no wonder you can't find this guy."

The officer wasn't amused. "I am taking this seriously and will file a report. There isn't much more we can do. A restraining order doesn't necessarily mean anything without proof. We don't have the manpower to follow Markowitz around everywhere he goes." The officer turned his attention back to Samantha. "We can put a tap on your phone, drive by more often, and see if we can get a glimpse of him violating the agreement. That's about all."

Reese continued to mutter, but Samantha knew the officer was right. Unless they could prove Dennis had left the note, he wouldn't be arrested.

Long after the officer had left and the pizza had been eaten, at least by Reese, Sam tried to send him home.

"I'd rather stay. Here, on the couch," he hastily added when she opened her mouth to argue. "Seriously, Samantha, I don't like the idea of you being here alone. Markowitz clearly knows where you live. What's to stop him from coming back later tonight?"

"The door outside is locked."

"Yeah, but that didn't stop him from finding a way in before."

All it would take was for Dennis to follow someone in who had a key, and they both knew it. She understood Reese was only being noble, and despite everything, she couldn't deny she liked having him near. Still, now that Dennis knew about Reese, she was more worried than ever. What was to stop Dennis from switching his threats from her to Reese? Or the other staff at Lifeline?

"Reese, go home. I need some time alone. Please try to understand."

Reluctantly, he stood. "I don't understand, but I'll go. Here's my number." He hastily scribbled it on a notepad. "Call me, no matter what time, I'll come right over."

"I will." She forced a smile. "See you at work, Reese."

When he brushed a quick kiss across her lips, it was all she could do to keep her hands at her sides, when she really wanted to grab him and hold on tight. He left, closing the door softly behind him.

Samantha double locked the door, then crossed over to her kitchen table and sank into a chair, burying her face in her hands.

She lied when she told Reese she'd see him at work. First thing Monday morning, she was going to meet with Dr. Jared O'Connor to request a reassignment.

She would miss flying, miss the responsibility of being a

flight physician, but leaving would be the best thing for the rest of the Lifeline staff.

Especially Reese.

~

Monday morning, she hurried into Lifeline, anxious to see Jared before he was swamped with other problems or was called out on a pediatric flight.

When she burst into his office, though, she found him already deep in conversation with Reese. Her stomach clenched painfully. She didn't doubt Reese was filling Jared in on what a huge security risk she'd become.

"Samantha." Reese quickly stood. "We were just talking about you."

"Really? I wouldn't have guessed." Her sarcasm made him wince. "But if you don't mind, I'd rather discuss my personal problems with Jared—alone."

"Samantha, sit down. Please." Jared's voice held enough authority to make her drop into the chair next to Reese. "Reese was filling me in on your ex-husband, and I must say I agree. Increasing security around here is the first order of business. Then we'll—"

"You don't need to do anything, Jared," Samantha interrupted. "Except find someone to replace me. I'm formally requesting a reassignment."

"Request denied." Jared didn't even blink. "There's a private investigator I know, a guy by the name of Brandon Rafter. I think he can help us find your ex."

What was he talking about? "You can't deny my request."

"Sure, I can." Jared smiled. "We've spent weeks training you. I can't replace you on a whim. Spring is coming, and when the weather warms, the trauma calls will double, if not triple. Besides, you're safer here where we already have specialized security than in another rotation."

"A whim?" her voice sharpened. "A transfer is best for *everyone's* safety."

"And it's better for you to stay." Jared's tone brooked no argument.

"Do you have a recent picture of Markowitz?" Reese wanted to know. "I think Brandon will need a photo to use during his investigation."

Sam reached up to rub her aching temples. They weren't listening to her. "I don't have a picture. I didn't keep anything of our marriage." She looked up at Jared. "Please think about this. I can stay long enough for you to train my replacement, then I'll leave."

"Last night you refused to run," Reese pointed out quietly. "Why don't you give Rafter a chance? He can do exactly what the police can't, follow Markowitz and catch him in the act. Once he's been arrested, you'll be safe."

Samantha could hardly imagine her life without Dennis the Menace looming in the background. The lure of possibly catching Dennis in the act was one she couldn't resist. Heaven knew, she wanted her life back.

But if anything happened to the Lifeline crew, especially to Reese, she wasn't sure she could live with yourself.

9

Indecision warred deep within. Sam hated feeling backed into a corner, but she finally nodded. "Okay. I won't run." At least, not yet, she silently amended. If the threats escalated, all bets were off.

As the men discussed hiring Brandon Rafter and outlining the private investigator's duties, a ray of hope filtered into her heart. Maybe they were onto something. Reese was right. This guy could do things the police couldn't. Why hadn't she thought of hiring a private investigator before now?

Because she'd been too busy running. The realization made her squirm. She'd worked so hard to get through medical school, to get accepted into an emergency medicine residency program. Now she was so close to graduating, to actually achieving success, that she'd chosen to keep running rather than to dig her heels in and fight.

"Since you don't have a picture, we'll need you to search for one on various social media sites," Jared said, interrupting her thoughts.

"Is that necessary? I mean, Dennis works at Weller Pharmaceuticals. His identity isn't a secret." She paused. "At least, he used to work there," she amended. "By now he may have a job with another company." It hadn't occurred to her that if Dennis had changed jobs to be with a different company, his territory may in fact include selling pharmaceutical products to the emergency medicine doctors here on campus. It would also explain why he'd met with Ben, her boss.

"Honestly, I think the social media is our best way to get a quick picture," Jared said. "Since you know what he looks like, it shouldn't take you too long to find him." Jared glanced at his watch. "You can use the computers here to do that search before you fly."

"I'm working nights tonight, so the search won't interfere with my ability to fly." Especially since searching social media probably wouldn't take long. "Anything else?"

"Once you have Markowitz's photo, you'll need to give all the information you have to Rafter so he can do his job." Reese stared intently at her face as if gauging her reaction.

She kept her expression impassive, not sure she was ready to forgive him for coming to Jared without even talking to her about it first. "I will."

"Great. It's settled. I'll call Rafter." Jared reached for his phone.

Samantha went over to use the computer in the Lifeline lounge. It didn't take her long to find a recent picture of Dennis Markowitz. Just seeing his face on the screen was enough to make her feel sick to her stomach. When she found a photo that included a close-up of his face, she printed it on the color printer sitting adjacent to the computer.

While she had been doing her searching, Jared must've asked Brandon Rafter to meet them at Lifeline. Jared asked

Sam to come into his office and introduced her to Brandon.

"It's nice to meet you," she said, offering her hand.

Brandon shook it solemnly. "Same here."

She looked pointedly at Jared, who thankfully left her alone in his office with the private investigator.

"I'm sorry we have to meet under these circumstances," Brandon said.

"Yeah. Well." She shifted awkwardly. "It's kind of a long story."

"I have time."

Sam found it surprisingly easy to talk to the quiet private investigator. He was young, maybe in his thirties, and handsome in a rugged sort of way. It wasn't easy for her to describe the events that led to the dissolution of her marriage, but Brandon didn't pass judgment or gush with sympathy. He was an excellent listener. At least, until the end when she asked about his fees. At that point, he abruptly stood.

"You'll have to discuss the bill with Dr. O'Connor," he told her hastily. "For now, you've given me exactly what I need to work with. This photo and the details of Dennis Markowitz's background should make it easy enough for me to find him."

Samantha stood, secretly annoyed with Jared. Was he really paying the bill or charging Lifeline for the private investigator's services? Either way wasn't right. This was her personal problem, no one else's. "You'll give me updates on what you find out?"

"As often as I can. Every few days to start, more often if I find something worth bothering you about," he promised.

Samantha knew he would, and the fact that Jared trusted him fueled her confidence. "Thanks."

Samantha returned to Lifeline a half hour prior to the start of her 1900 night shift. When she arrived, she sought out the printed version of the master schedule. Jared had given up on the electronic scheduling program after it had messed up his schedules, leaving him short a physician on a critical flight. The paper version was annoying but adequate. She looked at what she had coming up, only to notice Reese's name was written in alongside hers as the pilot on duty.

And not just for the upcoming shift. No, from the looks of things, he'd managed to manipulate his entire schedule to the point where it mirrored hers. Between Reese and Jared, she was beginning to feel her hard-earned independence slip away.

She found Reese in the debriefing room but didn't confront him right away. The off-going shift was still there, updating the oncoming shift on their day's activities.

"Weather is supposed to turn foggy later," Nate, the day shift pilot, informed them. "Hope it holds off for a while."

"Me, too," Samantha agreed. Night shifts were long enough on their own without adding flight delays. The minutes would crawl if they didn't get a chance to fly.

Ivan, the paramedic on duty with them, stifled a wide yawn. "I wouldn't mind a nap. Bethany is cutting teeth, so I didn't get much sleep today."

Sam smiled, having seen recent pictures of Ivan's beautiful six-month-old daughter. She imagined it would be a challenge to sleep during the day with the baby in the house. "Did you work last night, too?"

Wearily, Ivan nodded. "Didn't get much sleep the day before either." His tone was heavy with regret.

Their first flight call came in within the first hour of their shift. A single vehicle crash, car versus tree, made Sam suspect alcohol was involved. They weren't often called to routine accident sites, but from what they'd heard, the driver was on death's door. But that wasn't exactly the case.

When Sam arrived, the driver was unconscious with the strong odor of alcohol on his breath. As she performed a quick head-to-toe assessment while Ivan connected their patient to their equipment, she realized the initial call had been off base. Other than a large bump on his head, the patient was surprisingly uninjured.

The police at the scene wanted to arrest him, but Sam overrode their wishes, insisting he go to Trinity for evaluation first. After a light debate, the officers agreed to meet them in the emergency department. She knew, from personal experience, that they would hang around until a decision was made to admit him to the hospital or discharge him. If the decision was the latter, he wouldn't be allowed to go home but would be escorted by the officers straight to jail.

She and Ivan quickly loaded their patient into the chopper.

"How are things back there?" Reese asked as they headed toward Trinity.

"Fine. His head hurts too much for him to be a problem," Samantha replied. It wasn't unusual for patients to become combative, especially after sustaining a head injury under the influence of alcohol. But while her patient moaned frequently, he didn't thrash against the restraints.

They dropped him off at Trinity without mishap. The police arrived ten minutes later. Samantha and Ivan completed their paperwork, then returned to the helicopter.

Reese flew them back to the Lifeline hangar to wait for another call. True to his word, Ivan stretched out on the sofa in the lounge, taking advantage of the downtime to close his eyes for some desperately needed rest.

Samantha left him alone and returned to the debriefing room. She found Reese watching the satellite monitor.

"How's the weather holding?"

"Not too good. Cloud ceiling has dropped, with intermittent patches of fog. If it drops anymore, we won't be able to fly."

Sam hoped the clouds would cooperate, then turned her attention from the monitor. "I noticed you managed to finesse your schedule to match mine. Didn't I tell you I don't need a babysitter?"

"This is work, Samantha. I'm paid to fly, just as you are." She almost laughed at his comparison. As a resident, her pay was probably half what a pilot earned if not less. "So what if my shifts are the same as yours?" His gaze darkened, and he lowered his tone. "I prefer flying with you."

His simple admission made her breath catch in her throat. "I prefer flying with you, too, but that isn't the point."

"Then what is the point?" He stood, stepped closer, then reached up to smooth away a strand of hair that had escaped from her braid. "You need to clarify it for me because I must be dense."

Her protest died at the brush of his fingertips on her cheek. While she knew he was the wrong man at the wrong time, she yearned for more. His strength, his caring.

His touch.

"I don't want anything to happen to you." She finally pushed the words past her constricted throat. "I'm afraid Dennis may turn his anger toward you."

A feral grin tugged at his mouth. "Good. I hope he does just that."

"This isn't a joke," she said sharply, slapping her hand against his chest encased in the navy blue flight suit.

His smile vanished. His hands settled on her waist, pulling her toward him. "I wasn't joking, Samantha. I trained in the military, remember? I can handle myself. What I don't understand is why you can't trust me to protect you?"

"I trust you more than I've trusted any man." She didn't see the point of hiding the truth. "And you don't understand what it will do to me if Dennis tries to hurt you."

"Your ex-husband is too much of a coward to come after me." He drew her closer, and she didn't resist. His arms were strong, and the urge to rest her head on his chest was oh so tempting.

Maybe Reese would protect her physically, but who would protect her heart? "Reese," she whispered, splaying her hands wide on his chest. "What am I going to do with you?"

"Kiss me." He inched her closer until she was pressed against him, and his mouth lowered to hers. This was no tentative brush of his lips against hers. Nope, this time he flat-out kissed her, his mouth parting her lips, tongue delving deep, urging her to respond.

She did. A thrill of excitement zipped along her nerves as his taste went straight to her head faster than champagne. She'd never felt so on edge yet so protected at the same time. His hands stroked her back, cupped her shoulders, drawing her even closer.

Her mind went blank under his sensual kiss. When she couldn't breathe a minute longer, he released her mouth, tipped her head up, and trailed hot sizzling kisses down the line of her jaw. He pushed the fabric of her turtleneck sweater out of the way to press a kiss in the hollow of her throat.

Their pagers shrilled simultaneously. With a low groan and obvious reluctance, Reese lifted his head. Sam blinked and tried to focus.

"Multivehicle car crash," Sam said, reading the message on her pager. "Fifty miles north of here. I need to make sure Ivan is up."

"Don't. We are not responding to this call." Reese turned toward the phone.

"What?" Sam swung her gaze toward the monitor to see if she'd missed something. "The cloud ceiling hasn't moved any lower. And the peds crew is out on a call."

He ignored her. "Paramedic base, we are in yellow flying conditions. We are not responding at this time." Reese's voice was calm as he gave the directive. "You might want to contact the peds crew to let them know the changing conditions here. They may want to stay put for a while."

"Reese, I don't want to fly in poor conditions any more than you do, but are you sure there isn't a way for us to respond?" The aborted flight was still fresh in her mind, but it wasn't even snowing, just a low cloud ceiling. "Those people need help. A few minutes ago, you said if the ceiling drops lower, we won't fly. Well, it hasn't dropped lower, it's the same." She could not keep the frustration from her voice. "I think we need to respond to this call."

"No. You don't understand the weather conditions like a pilot does." His calm voice didn't seem to betray any hint of regret, which only ticked her off.

"You're the one who changed his tune," she argued, her voice rising with anger. "So don't tell me I don't understand.

If this is your attitude, maybe I'm better off flying with Nate or one of the other pilots."

Reese's dark brown eyes turned black. "You don't know the risks. I do. The weather can change in a heartbeat. Have you read the detailed crash reports after a fatality? Especially when one of the crew members that died happened to be someone you cared about?"

The news caught her by the throat. Reese had always seemed cool and calm and in control. But he wasn't cool now. "No," she whispered.

"Well, I have. It isn't pretty." Reese jammed his hands into the pockets of his flight suit. He hunched his shoulders as if embarrassed by his outburst. Calmer now, he continued, "The wind is coming in from the north, right over the lake. The crash scene is also fifty miles to the north. When the warmer air over the lake hits the cold north wind, the fog will get worse. Remember the other night, when we were suddenly in the middle of a snowstorm? Lake Michigan makes the weather unpredictable. That's why I turned down the flight. For your safety, mine, and Ivan's."

"Oh." She felt small, petty for arguing with him about something she knew so little about. Clearly Reese was the best one to make the decision either way. "You're right. As the pilot, you should be the one making the call."

"Yes, but it's not always that straightforward." Reese rubbed his eyes, then leaned his hips against the edge of the desk. "Some pilots would fly in this weather. I'm just not one of them. But you should have the right to decide for yourself, too. Every crew member should."

Sam didn't know quite what to say to that. But she remembered the sad look in his eyes a few days ago, and when combined with the most recent comments, the truth clicked. "Who was she?" she asked.

He glanced away. "What do you mean?"

"The woman you cared about and lost to a crash." The signs were so clear now that she knew to look for them. Everyone joked about Reese peering over Mitch's shoulder as their mechanic tinkered with the chopper engine and how he took flying safety so seriously. But none of them had understood why. If there had been any rumors about Reese's past, she hadn't heard them.

He was silent for so long she thought he wasn't going to answer. "Valerie. We were engaged to be married. My best friend, Greg Hasking, was the pilot. The physician on board was Jim Whelan, a guy who left behind a wife and two kids."

Dear heaven above. Sorrow washed over her. Samantha couldn't imagine how the poor physician's widow must have felt, losing her husband so young. And Reese. How had he survived, losing two people so close to him? His best friend and his fiancée? "They all died?"

Reese slowly nodded. "They were flying to a hospital to pick up a critically ill patient and got caught in a snowstorm in the mountains of Colorado. I—they shouldn't have been flying. The weather was too risky."

"I'm sorry, Reese." She longed to comfort him, to soothe his pain. "I'm so sorry for your loss."

He shrugged lightly. "Valerie knew the risks, and she loved to fly. I just wish I had been there, like I was supposed to be. But I had switched shifts with Greg."

She winced, knowing that fact would have only added to Reese's guilt. "It's not your fault."

"I should've been there." His flat tone betrayed the depth of his grief.

Sam ached for him, for what he'd lost. For the physician's wife and children. Thinking about Ivan's wife and young daughter hit hard. She never should have doubted Reese's expertise when it came to flying. She summoned a sad smile. "You're here now. And it may be selfish of me, but I'm glad." She placed a hesitant hand on his arm. "I'm very glad, Reese."

"Samantha." His voice turned husky when she slid her hand up and wrapped her arms around his neck to pull him toward her in a gesture meant to give comfort. He dipped his head to rest on her shoulder, his arms loose around her waist. "I'm glad, too," he whispered against her collarbone.

Her heart soared, and she blinked away unexpected tears. She threaded her hands through his hair, enjoying the silky texture against her fingertips.

His grip tightened at her waist, and he turned his face into her neck. "You smell so good. Like Christmas every day."

She smiled. As he pressed his lips against the side of her neck, she clutched at his shoulders.

He groaned low in his throat and lifted his head, taking several gulping breaths. "We need to stop. I'm not sure how much of this I can take."

"But I like kissing you." Sam boldly met his gaze.

His eyes widened in a way that would've been comical if she hadn't wanted him so badly. "There's no rush, Samantha. You aren't ready for a relationship, remember?"

"And you were the one to point out how it was already too late," she reminded him right back. Reaching up, she cupped his cheek in her hand. "I care about you, Reese."

He kissed her again, clutching her close. After a long moment, he lifted his head. "Samantha, I want you to be sure," he said finally, looking directly into her eyes. "Your career is important to you, and boards are only a few short months away. For now, I'm content to simply hold you. To be there for you. To comfort you."

The blazing hunger in his gaze was a far cry from his chaste words, and Samantha was touched by his willingness to wait. Had she ever met a man who'd put her needs first? Medical school had been competitive, each student vying for the highest grades to ensure the best residency match. When she'd married Dennis, and he'd dropped out within the first two months, things had gone from competitive to controlling.

Yet here was Reese, tense with desire but willing to do whatever was better for her. Not controlling her, not trying to compete with her career, but supporting her decisions, whatever they may be.

"I'm sure about you, Reese. I've never felt this way before."

Reese laughed and groaned at the same time. "That's a crazy thing to say when we have a long shift ahead of us."

Samantha's smile held a hint of humor. "Tired of talking to me already?"

Reese brought his hands up to cup her face, deepening the kiss for a long moment until they both needed to breathe. "Never. You are so beautiful, Samantha." He kissed her again, gently this time, as if she were the greatest treasure in the world.

Overcome with awe, she blinked away sudden tears. So this was how love was supposed to feel.

Kind, gentle, sweet, and caring.

DURING THE LONG hours of the night, Reese had checked the radar frequently, updating the paramedic base on the nasty turn of the weather. Now dawn was only a short hour away. During the night, Reese and Samantha had spent their hours together cuddling, kissing, and talking.

She'd opened up more about her disastrous marriage, and he'd told her about Valerie and how he'd always known his best friend was a daredevil pilot.

Reese had broken his rule by getting involved with Samantha. They'd only talked and kissed, but he'd never felt as close to another woman as he did with Samantha.

He glanced at where she was curled in a chair, asleep. "Samantha, you better get up." He gently shook her shoulder. "I hear Ivan up and about in the lounge."

"Okay." She smiled at him, her beautiful smoky gray eyes heavy lidded with sleep. "I'm awake."

Deciding it was best not to kiss her again, since Ivan could come in any moment, Reese walked over to check the weather monitor. The threat of fog had turned into a full-blown snowstorm within the past several hours. The howling wind and swirling snow had dropped visibility to mere inches. Needless to say, no one at Lifeline would be flying anywhere in the next few hours.

After updating the paramedic base and verifying that the Lifeline peds crew would leave the chopper at Children's Memorial and catch a ride from a car service back to the base, Reese logged into his email. The first item to capture his attention was an alert from Pilots Inc., the voluntary organization of helicopter rescue pilots sharing medical air flight information across the country.

"Crash alert. Chicago's Air Angels suffered a fatal helicopter crash at zero two hundred hours this morning. Fatalities included the entire crew; pilot, flight nurse, and flight physician. Our prayers go out to the crew's family and friends."

Stunned, Reese stared at the message. There were

bound to be other factors surrounding the crash, but one thing was for sure. Chicago's weather often mirrored theirs as both cities bordered Lake Michigan.

The Chicago Air Angel pilot had crashed flying in weather Reese had refused to fly in.

10

When Samantha came over, Reese quickly minimized his email, instinctively wanting to protect her from the horror of the crash. Yet, logically, he knew she was far better off knowing the true risk.

"You didn't make any coffee?" Sam's voice echoed with disappointment.

"Sorry. I don't drink coffee." Changing his mind about keeping the truth a secret, he double clicked on the email icon and brought the crash message back up on the screen. With a couple of keystrokes, he printed out the message. He heard water running as she prepared to brew a fresh pot of coffee. When she finished, he cleared his throat to get her attention. "I have some bad news."

"Bad news?" Her tone was panicked, and she turned toward him so fast she lost her balance, leaning heavily against the counter. "Dennis?"

"No, sorry. Not that." He could have kicked himself for not realizing that's where her brain would go. Although, he wasn't sure the crash news was any better. He handed her a copy of his email message. "Better sit down before reading this."

"Oh, no." She took a seat beside him. Her eyes raked over the message, then lifted to meet his. "Reese, this is awful. Chicago is only about ninety miles from here."

"I know." He dropped heavily into the seat beside the satellite monitor. "Too close to home."

"This could have been us." Agitated now, she jumped to her feet and began to pace the short length of the room. "I was insisting we fly to the crash scene last night. If we had gone, we could have died. Just like this."

Reese couldn't deny the grim truth. "There may be mitigating factors we are not aware of," he pointed out. "The FAA will do a thorough investigation before making a final determination."

"A final determination of what?" Ivan asked, scratching his chin as he entered the debriefing room. "Samantha, thanks for making coffee."

"On the cause of the crash." Reese knew Ivan had been flying long enough to understand the risks.

Ivan's expression turned somber. "Who crashed?"

"Air Angel." Reese handed him the message. "Last night at zero two hundred hours."

"What were the flying conditions?" Ivan asked as his gaze flicked over the email.

"Patchy fog but a cold wind coming in from the north." Reese filled him in on the events of last night, including the decision to keep one chopper at Children's Memorial rather than risk a return flight. "You were sleeping so soundly we didn't wake you."

"Thanks." His white teeth flashed in a grin. "My wife will

appreciate your thoughtfulness. I can help with Bethany today, rather than trying to sleep in snatches."

Reese nodded, not about to mention how he and Samantha had spent the night cuddling and chatting, benefiting from Ivan's exhaustion.

"Is Jared in yet?" Reese asked.

Ivan shook his head. "I think he's going to be a little late today. Shelly has her first doctor's appointment this morning." When Reese's eyes widened in alarm, the paramedic hastened to reassure him. "Haven't you heard? She's pregnant."

His expression cleared. "No, I hadn't heard. I'm happy for them, though."

"The baby pool will be up soon." Ivan helped himself to coffee.

"Shelly, the peds flight nurse?" Samantha halted her pacing to turn and look at them. "I knew she married Jared a few months ago and that they both still fly. Now she's pregnant?" She looked alarmed at the thought.

Clearly, the news of the fatal crash was still too fresh and painful. "Knowing Jared, he won't allow Shelly to keep flying once she's further along." Reese did his best to console her.

"Yeah, but you're assuming Shelly will listen." Ivan pointed out dryly.

Since Reese already knew how stubborn flight nurse Shelly O'Connor could be, he held his tongue. "Samantha, try to relax. Lifeline has an excellent thirty-five-year crash-free history. Safety is our prime concern."

"I know." She tried to smile but failed miserably. "At least, I do now. I'm glad you insisted on remaining grounded last night."

Reese rubbed his hands over his face and wished he'd acquired a taste for coffee. He could use the kick of caffeine to help dissolve the fog in his brain. The decision he'd made had been gut instinct more than anything. He could have just as easily agreed to fly. He'd been honest with Samantha last night; the weather could always change without warning. The day they'd tried to fly to Two Rivers, only to head back because of the weather, was proof of how even the best pilot could find himself facing poor flying conditions.

The truth was difficult to deny. Anyone could crash. Reese knew he could lose Samantha, the same way he'd lost Valerie.

Long after Ivan had gone home, Reese buried his head in paperwork he'd neglected while waiting for Jared. He had a plan that he needed Jared's approval to implement.

Samantha had given him a strange look when he'd told her he needed to work late today. He knew he was treating her badly, especially after the closeness they'd shared during the night, but the news of the crash had shaken him more than he'd wanted to admit. Putting some distance between him and Samantha seemed prudent.

He heard voices in the hallway outside the debriefing room and wondered if Jared had finally arrived. Piling the reports in a neat stack, he grabbed his proposal and pushed away from the desk.

The voices came from Jared's office. He paused outside the partially open door, trying to figure out who was in there. In a heartbeat, he recognized Samantha's lyrical voice.

"What's your plan?" Jared asked.

"My only plan for the moment is to ace my boards," Reese heard Samantha respond. "But after that I'm thinking of moving to the West Coast, to the San Diego area. My parents still live there, even though my siblings are scattered across the country."

Reese felt a sharp pain in his chest as if he'd been punched. Samantha planned to move after graduation? Funny, she hadn't mentioned that to him.

"Let me know what you decide. I'd be happy to write you a glowing letter of recommendation," Jared was saying. "In the meantime, I'll keep you posted on whatever information Rafter comes up with."

"Thanks. I appreciate it."

Reese steadied himself on the doorframe, Samantha's words beating against his temple. When he sensed their conversation was over, he pulled himself together, rapped his knuckles against the frame, and poked his head to the doorway. "Jared? Do you have a minute?"

"Sure." Jared and Samantha stood up. "Talk to you later, Samantha."

She nodded and smiled at Reese, an unspoken question in her gaze. She was wondering what he was doing there while he was trying to figure out why she hadn't told him about her plans to move after graduation. "See you later, Reese."

She said it as a question, and he knew she was wondering if she'd see him sooner rather than later. Considering how he'd badgered her to share meals with him, he understood. Yet Reese couldn't bring himself to answer. He also didn't stop her from leaving, as much as he wanted to. Even though her future plans had shaken him, he knew Markowitz was still out there. He trusted Brandon Rafter, but the need to follow Samantha home was strong.

He forced himself to let her go.

"What's on your mind, Reese?" Jared settled in behind his desk.

"A team approach to flying." He handed Jared his quickly written proposal before sitting across from him. "Did you hear about the Air Angel crash last night?"

Jared frowned. "No."

Reese quickly filled him in. "I'm a cautious pilot by nature, but not every pilot sees weather conditions exactly the same way. With each takeoff, safety measures will only go so far. You know as well as I do there are many factors outside our control."

"I'm with you so far," Jared agreed.

"I'm proposing that each team member has the right to decide if they feel comfortable flying in dicey weather conditions. If even one person has reservations, the flight is called off. The captain doesn't have veto rights, insisting it's safe to fly."

"Interesting proposal," Jared murmured, skimming the information Reese had handed him. "Have any other air transport companies initiated a similar policy?"

"Not that I'm aware of." Reese couldn't lie. "In fact, companies that are in it for profit will push the limit on flying conditions. Air Angel just happens to be a commercial company."

Jared thoughtfully nodded. "We are fortunate to be subsidized by the area hospitals and the state, allowing us to retain our nonprofit status." He tapped the proposal. "I like this, Reese. I say we implement your plan immediately. We'll track the flight refusals and see how it goes."

Relief loosened the tight bands around his chest. "Thanks, Jared. I appreciate your support."

"I have as much invested in this program as you do,"

Jared pointed out. His gaze dropped to the proposal. "In some ways, more."

It didn't take a genius to figure out Jared was thinking about his wife and unborn child. "I know." He cleared his throat. "I take it there's no news from Rafter yet?"

Jared shook his head. "Not yet. He's dug into Markowitz's background, though, and has staked out his condo. I'm sure we'll hear something soon. At least, when he makes a move toward Samantha, we'll know."

A fresh wave of guilt flooded Reese. He should have followed her home. "Keep me posted, too."

If Jared thought his request was strange, he didn't let on. "I will. Get some sleep."

Reese drove home, knowing sleep would be a long time coming. He actually pulled into the parking space next to Samantha's before realizing what he'd done. With a mental head-slap, he threw his truck in reverse and headed to the next building over.

Inside, he couldn't dredge up his usually insatiable appetite. His team approach to flying might have saved Valerie, but not if she'd been willing to go. Oddly enough, the memory of Valerie didn't hurt the way it used to. Samantha's plan for her future came floating back to him. He should have followed his instincts and stayed far away from her. The time they would have together could be measured in days, maybe months, before she'd leave.

Pain thickened his throat as realization dawned. Losing Samantha would be far worse than when he'd lost Valerie. Because Valerie hadn't had a choice. He'd always known she'd loved him.

He didn't have Samantha's love. He knew she cared for him, but that didn't change the fact that she planned to walk away.

Leaving him, behind.

SAMANTHA SHOULD HAVE BEEN EXHAUSTED, but she couldn't sleep. Not that sleeping in the bright light of day had ever been easy. She'd struggled when other residents she knew could drop off no matter what time of day it was.

The problem right now was Reese. The night in the debriefing room where they talked for hours had been wonderful. Better than wonderful. But in the morning, his whole attitude had changed.

She couldn't really blame him. News of the Air Angel crash was enough to ruin anyone's mood. But she couldn't help but wonder about the woman Reese had loved. The woman he'd asked to marry him. To be jealous of a dead woman was utterly foolish, but her heart twisted painfully anyway.

Had he felt guilty for kissing her? Looking back, she didn't think so. Reese's demeanor hadn't changed until this morning, when he'd read of the news of the crash. Obviously, he was still torn up inside over losing his fiancée. What had she been like, this woman who still had a hold on Reese's heart? She tossed her arm over her eyes, trying to block out the endless questions along with the light. What did it matter what the woman had been like? Reese wasn't in Colorado anymore. He was here at Lifeline.

But he had left his heart behind with a woman who had died in the mountains.

How ironic that the first man she'd grown to love and trust in the years since she'd mistaken Dennis's companionship for love wasn't in a position to return those feelings in kind.

A THUNK outside her bedroom window woke her out of a sound sleep. Groggily, she blinked, trying to read the luminous numbers on her clock. Six in the evening. She'd only managed to sleep for a few hours.

Sliding her feet into slippers, Samantha crossed the room. With a frown, she peered through the window. Had she heard something out there, or had it been her imagination? Since learning about her smashed car battery, she tended to suspect Dennis lurking around every corner.

The shrill ringing of her phone drew her attention, and she immediately stepped away from the window. The moment she moved, a loud crash burst from behind her. She instinctively screamed and threw herself to the floor.

She heard a shout, followed by a yell somewhere outside. Samantha raised her head from the floor, glancing around in fear. Her bedroom window was broken, a gaping hole in the center surrounded by jagged glass. The opening wasn't large enough for a person, she noted in relief. Had Dennis struck again?

Her phone was still ringing, so she jumped to her feet and dashed over to the kitchen where the phone was charging on the counter. The number on the screen was blocked, but she still answered. "Hello?"

Too late. The mystery person on the other end of the line hung up. Shivering with the cold February air flowing freely through the broken window, she found her Lifeline jacket and slipped it on over her flannel pajamas. Shaking, she tried to decide what to do first. Call the police? Call to have her broken window repaired? Take care of the broken glass splattered around her bedroom?

Edging down the hall, she stood in the doorway of her bedroom. Lying in the center of her bed was a large, heavy brick. Wrapped around the brick was some sort of brown paper. Even from this distance she could see the message written on the note, addressed to her.

She didn't want to read it, knowing the note would be more of the same. *Come home, where you belong.* Turning from the mess in her room, she returned to the kitchen. Seeing the brick had helped her make a decision. Police first, then repair the window.

She'd already called the police when she heard more noise from outside. The car engine, then the slam of car door. She went tense. Had Dennis come back?

"Samantha!" She heard a male shout her name a moment before there was pounding on her apartment door. "Are you all right? Open up."

"Reese?" She peered through the peephole, surprised and very relieved to see him standing there. She opened the door. "How did you get into the building?"

"Followed someone. Are you all right?" He came forward and cupped her face in his hands, brushing his thumbs over her cheeks. "Brandon called me when you didn't answer your phone, told me he saw Markowitz outside your building."

The wild look in his eye belayed her fear. "I'm fine. But my window isn't."

"I thought it was cold in here." Reese pressed his mouth against hers in a brief, hard kiss. Then he pulled back to look around the apartment. "What happened?"

"A noise outside woke me up." His kiss rattled her brains, and she frowned in order to concentrate. "I, uh, got up and went over to the window to see if anyone was out there. Then my phone started to ring, so I stepped away intending to answer it. I heard a crash and hit the floor." She was embarrassed at her reaction, cowering in fear instead of facing the danger head-on. "Someone hurled a brick through my window."

"Someone? You mean Markowitz." Reese's hands tightened on her arms. "Samantha, he could've hit you. The next time you hear a noise, don't go anywhere near the window."

"I won't." The closeness of her near miss, along with the cold air, made her teeth chatter.

"Did you call the police?"

She nodded. "They're on their way."

Reese led her over to the sofa, urging her to sit. "Stay here. I'll check out the damage."

Sam clasped her hands together to stop them from trembling. "I know Dennis is probably long gone, but I'll need the police report to pay for the broken window."

He disappeared down the hall toward her bedroom. Samantha sat for a moment, then realized she was doing it again. She was letting others take control of her life. Jumping to her feet, she followed Reese.

"Stay back." His voice was harsh. "You'll cut yourself. There's glass everywhere."

Since her feet felt like twin blocks of ice, even wearing slippers, she knew she wouldn't feel a sharp edge of glass until it was too late. She hovered in the doorway, surveying the mess in her room. "How am I going to get the glass out of the carpet?"

Reese's normally calm features reflected his seething anger. "I don't know, but we can't touch anything the cops may be able to use as evidence. I hope Brandon managed to get some evidence, too." He turned away from the window. "Tell me what you need so I can get it for you."

Sam directed him to where her shoes, socks, jeans, and sweaters were located. Despite how they'd cuddled and talked the night before, her face grew pink as he went through her dresser drawers, pulling out the items she'd requested, including clean underwear and a bra. Once he'd retrieved her things, she took them gratefully and disappeared into the bathroom to change.

She felt more in control when she emerged, fully dressed, a few minutes later. The police arrived fast, the broken window rating a higher threat than her earlier note. While she answered their questions, she noticed Reese talking on a cell phone.

"Was that Brandon?" she asked, breaking away from the police officer's questions.

Reese nodded. "Yeah. I called and asked him to return. He's on his way. He said he took off after Markowitz, but the guy managed to slip away."

She couldn't hide the sharp stab of disappointment. So close, they had been so close to nailing Dennis in the act. Sam forced herself to remain calm. "Next time, I guess."

"There shouldn't have to be a next time." Reese's frustration mirrored hers. He'd raked his hands through his hair so many times the strands stood on end, sticking out of his head at all angles. She suspected he'd recently woken up from sleep himself. "I thought Brandon was better than this. I can't believe he let the jerk to get away."

Samantha secretly felt the same way, although she knew Dennis was craftier than most people believed. Underestimating him was only too easy. She'd married him thinking he was a great guy with similar goals and desires to hers.

She'd been wrong. And right now, she was finding out just how wrong. The police combed her apartment, taking photographs of the master bedroom and dusting for prints on the wall outside of her window and on the brick itself. After a few minutes, her buzzer sounded.

Hesitantly, she crossed the room. "Yes?"

"It's Rafter."

"Come on in." She pushed the button to release the outside lock, then opened her apartment door.

Rafter didn't look upset to have lost his man. In fact, a broad grin creased his features. In his hands he held several photographs.

"We got him." He displayed the photos on her kitchen table. "I have a digital camera and portable printer in my car. I printed these out a few minutes ago."

Reese crossed over to take a look. Samantha caught her breath. The pictures were amazingly clear. Brandon had caught a clear photo of Dennis outside her window, holding what looked like the brick in his hand.

"Great." Reese clapped a hand on Brandon's shoulder. "I have to admit I was upset you'd allowed him to get away."

"The pictures had to come first, or trust me, I would've had him. I honestly didn't see the brick in his hand at first. I didn't know he'd planned to chuck it through her window until I saw the swing of his arm. I called Samantha to warn her. But at least we have the evidence needed for the police to arrest him."

Samantha lifted her gaze from the grim photos. The officer who'd questioned her entered the room, the pictures drawing his attention.

"Markowitz is in clear violation of his restraining order, and more, this shows his attempted assault." Rafter looked pleased with himself.

The officer picked up the picture of Dennis holding the brick mere seconds before he'd launched it through her window. "These are good. I'll send a team to stake out his condo, authorizing his arrest."

Samantha pressed a shaking hand over her heart. It was over. Dennis the Menace would be arrested soon, and the nightmare would come to an end.

11

Reese stared at the window he'd boarded up in Samantha's room. Like winter wasn't dark enough, he thought ruefully. With the plywood nailed across the opening, there would be no light streaming in. Raking a hand through his hair, he stepped back. The police had finally left and so had Rafter. The PI still planned to stake out Samantha's building, but Reese seriously doubted that Markowitz would show.

He'd be too busy getting arrested.

Still, he didn't like leaving Samantha here alone. But how to convince her to move in temporarily with him? After their stilted conversation earlier this morning, he knew he'd botched things badly. He was probably the last guy on earth, other than Markowitz, she wanted to spend time with.

"I suppose you're hungry." Samantha entered the room, surveying his handiwork. "Thanks for fixing my window."

If only he could fix more than the stupid window. "No problem. It's the least I can do."

She lifted a brow. "Why is that? My broken window is hardly your fault."

He sighed and met her gaze. "I guess it's my way of apologizing for the way I acted this morning."

With a shrug, she glanced away. "It's all right. I can only imagine the horrible memories you must have of the crash."

It wasn't just the crash, but he couldn't bring himself to bring up the subject of her plans to move to San Diego after graduation. Not her fault that he'd begun to fall for her. He hadn't expected to feel this much for any woman ever again. There was a brief silence before he added, "I didn't get the chance to tell you how much I enjoyed spending the night talking with you."

Her gaze shot to his. "I thought you were having second thoughts about the time we spent together."

Slowly, he shook his head. "No. You've made me feel alive, Samantha. I could never regret spending time with you." No matter how short that time might be, he thought to himself.

A hopeful smile bloomed on her face. "I'm glad."

"Will you come back to my place? We can pick up something to eat on the way." He held his breath, prepared for her refusal.

"I have to work in the morning," she hedged. Then she laughed and shook her head. "And since you've switched your schedule to match mine, so do you."

"I know. I'm asking you to stay with me at least until Markowitz is caught and arrested." He'd missed being with her. He missed talking with her. And most of all he missed kissing her.

"Reese, I don't need protecting anymore," she said as if reading his mind. "For all we know, the police have already arrested Dennis."

He wasn't so sure about that but hoped the police would

find him soon. But that wasn't the only reason he wanted her to come by his place. He wanted to touch her, to pull her into his arms. He forced himself to keep his hands at his sides. "I know. I'm not asking you to stay just because of Markowitz. I'm asking because I want to spend time with you."

"You do?" Samantha raised one eyebrow questioningly. There was a hint of uncertainty in her gaze.

He swallowed hard, knowing he didn't dare push her. "Only to talk, Samantha."

She tipped her head to the side, a secret smile playing along her lips. "Just to talk, huh?"

He had no clue what to say to that. Especially since he knew this—whatever was growing between them—was only temporary. "I like spending time with you, Samantha. Just being with you is more than enough."

She smiled wryly and nodded. "Okay, Reese. Since you are being such a gentleman, I'll take you up on your kind offer. I can't deny that the thought of staying here alone now that Dennis knows where I am isn't very appealing. It might be better to stay someplace else until we know he's in jail."

He let out his breath in a soundless sigh. For once she wasn't going to argue with him. "My sofa is fairly comfortable."

She didn't move, and he wondered if she was having second thoughts.

"Why don't you pack a bag?" he suggested. "Again, no pressure, but the morning will go more smoothly if you have everything you need for work."

She agreed, and he couldn't help smiling as he drove the short distance between her apartment building and his.

He was crazy to continue allowing himself to become

involved, but at the same time, he couldn't seem to stay away.

SAMANTHA COULDN'T BELIEVE how easy it was to spend time with Reese. The small apartment created a level of intimacy, but Reese never took advantage of the situation. Even though she wouldn't have minded a kiss or two, she knew that it was better that they kept things friendly.

Reese called Rafter and asked if Dennis had been arrested yet. Unfortunately, the news wasn't good. So far, the police hadn't been able to arrest Dennis because he hadn't gone home to his condo.

She didn't want to think about where Dennis might be staying. She told herself it was only a matter of time. Her ex-husband couldn't hide forever.

The sofa was comfortable, and she slept good knowing she was safe. There was a bit of awkwardness in the morning as they took turns in the bathroom, but he did his best to stay out of her way.

Reese offered to drive them to work, pointing out that they lived in the same apartment complex and that it was ridiculous to drive two cars from their respective buildings to the Lifeline hangar.

The only problem with accepting a ride from Reese was that she didn't like the idea of the two of them showing up together. The staff at Lifeline was small, and gossip spread quickly.

It was enough to have her shaking her head. "Honestly, Reese, I'd rather take my own car." Samantha braced herself for an argument.

Reese frowned, indicating he didn't like her decision,

but he didn't try to talk her out of it either. "All right. But at least let me drive you to your car."

Sam relaxed. She knew Reese wasn't like Dennis, needing to control her every move. The way he gave in to her wishes warmed her heart. Maybe there was something to this relationship thing after all.

She drove to Lifeline with Reese following close behind. She had to smile at how he didn't so much as let one car come between them.

The sky was clear, but the wind was sharp as they headed inside the hangar a little later. Andrew was the paramedic on duty with her again today. Since Sam entered first, followed a few minutes later by Reese, he didn't notice anything different about how they acted toward each other.

While she knew it was foolish, she didn't want to announce the change in her relationship with Reese to the whole world. Especially since there really wasn't a relationship. Just a few kisses, okay, more than a few hot kisses, but nothing more. Besides, she didn't know if he was truly over Valerie.

The night shift gave their debriefing, anxious to leave and go home. Less than an hour later, their first call came in.

"Fifty-year-old male fell through the ice on Lake Minooka while ice fishing," Andrew announced.

"Did they get him out?" she asked.

"Not yet."

"Let's get there, maybe we can help."

The three of them grabbed their helmets and dashed for the chopper. Lake Minooka was a good fifteen-minute flight away, and in cases of severe hypothermia, every second counted.

Samantha nervously clutched the roll bar and held her

breath when Reese lifted the chopper off the ground. She hadn't expected to feel so nervous about flying. It wasn't as if she didn't trust Reese, because she did. Still, several minutes went by before she could pry her fingers off the roll bar.

"Hey, doc. You okay?" Andrew asked, concern darkening his gaze.

"Something wrong, Samantha?" Reese immediately asked from the pilot's seat, picking up on Andrew's comment.

"Nothing is wrong. I'm fine." Samantha maintained an even tone. "Honest. Just get us to the scene, Reese, as quickly as possible."

"Roger."

The chopper banked right, and Samantha was relieved when her initial nervousness faded. How had Reese managed to get into the cockpit again after Valerie had crashed? Flying after something like that was true bravery.

"We are coming up on Lake Minooka, but we need to find a place to land that's not too close to the lake." Reese's deep voice flowed through her headset.

She frowned. "I don't understand. Why can we get close to the lake?"

"The noise and wind speed of the blades could break up the rest of the ice," Reese explained. "If the rescue crew is still on the ice, they could all fall in."

Not good. Suppressing a shiver, Samantha peered out her window at the scene below. "How much room do you need, Reese? There's a road about one hundred yards from the lake to the south. If there was a way to block traffic, would that work?"

"I see it, and yes, the location is perfect. I'll radio the base."

They wasted precious minutes as they relayed the information to the officials at the scene who agreed to set up a road block. Reese finally landed the chopper. Andrew and Samantha didn't waste any time.

They were both breathing heavily when they pulled up at the group of rescue workers gathered around the lake. "Did you get him out?" Sam asked.

"Yeah, but he doesn't have a pulse. The firefighters are working on him now."

Sam elbowed her way to the patient's side. "How long was he under?"

"Less than ten minutes. The icy water might have worked in our favor, though." With a nod, she indicated she understood. The body required less oxygen when submerged in icy water. But anything close to ten minutes was still a very long time.

"Hey, I think I feel a pulse." The firefighter looked up at her.

Samantha placed her fingers along the carotid artery as well. She nodded. "I do, too."

"Let's get some meds into him before we lose it again."

She helped the firefighters while Andrew prepared the gurney. The patient's heart rate had returned, but the rhythm was hardly regular.

"Get the Amiodarone ready, and make sure the defibrillator is charged up. We could lose his heart rhythm at any moment."

Thankfully, the firefighters had placed an intraosseous IV.

"Andrew, do you have the fluid warmer on?"

"You bet." He finished switching all the equipment, including the IV. On the count of three, they lifted the patient and swung him onto the gurney.

"Let's go." Samantha took a deep breath, preparing for the long hike to the chopper.

"Use the ambulance." One of the firefighters gestured to the waiting vehicle. "You'll get there much faster. This guy has to weigh at least a hundred kilos."

"Thanks." Samantha gratefully accepted his offer.

With the help of the ambulance, they reached the helicopter in record time. Reese had the blades whirling, ready to go.

She and Andrew loaded the patient through the hatch. Andrew gestured for her to follow the patient inside, then closed the door after her. He jogged around to get in along the right side.

Once Andrew was settled in beside her, she switched on her mic. "We're good to go back here, Reese."

"Roger. Base, we're preparing for lift-off."

Samantha busied herself with hooking up the warming blanket and spreading it out to cover their patient. Then she checked the medication while Andrew began filling out the paperwork.

"I'm losing his rhythm here," she warned. "He's having tons of PVCs. I'm increasing the Amiodarone."

"Got it." Andrew jotted down the notations, then reached over to power up the defibrillator. "Let me know if you want to cardiovert."

"I will." Samantha increased the medication, then watched the effects on the monitor. "We still have a pulse, and a borderline yet currently stable blood pressure. Let's wait to see what the medication can do."

"Is everything all right back there?" Reese asked. "Do you need me to divert our course?"

"Negative. We are holding our own. At least for the moment." Samantha wondered how Reese seemed able to read every inflection of her tone. Although he was seated in the cockpit, she always felt as if he were right beside her.

There was no time to be afraid of flying as they neared Trinity Medical Center. "Reese, radio ahead and tell them I need a hot unload."

"Will do." She barely listened as Reese did as she'd requested. "ETA roughly five minutes."

"Come on, hang on," she murmured, giving her patient another bolus of Amiodarone. She wondered if they may have underestimated the patient's weight. For all they knew, he could be closer to one hundred and twenty kilos. It wasn't always easy to estimate a patient's weight.

"Getting ready to land," Reese informed them.

The minutes had never gone so fast. "We're ready."

As soon as Reese landed, Andrew jumped out to release the hatch. Between them, they pulled out their patient and set him down. The emergency department staff were waiting as requested on the helipad. The extra hands were helpful.

"Core temp is still only thirty-one degrees Celsius. And he still having a lot of PVCs," Samantha shouted as they wheeled him inside.

The elevator ride down to the emergency department seemed longer than the flight from the lake had been.

"Thank heavens, you guys got there when you did, or he wouldn't have any chance at all," one of the ED nurses commented.

Samantha wordlessly agreed. They wheeled the patient into the closest trauma bay and continued to work on him while another nurse called up to the ICU to arrange a bed. Samantha and Andrew stepped aside. Their role in saving this ice fisherman's life was over, but he wasn't out of the woods yet.

The nurse had been right. Flying was probably safer than ground transport, even in rough weather conditions. There were far more car crashes than flight disasters.

And it was clear that without Lifeline this guy wouldn't have stood a chance.

"Everything go okay?" Reese asked, once they'd climbed back on board.

"Yeah, for now. He's in good hands," Samantha told him.

"I need to refuel before heading back to the hangar."

"Sounds good."

The extra trip added twenty minutes before they arrived back at Lifeline. Inside the debriefing room and out of Andrew's earshot, Reese caught Samantha's arm. "Hey. Are you really all right?"

"I'm fine." She tried to shrug, but Reese only tightened his grip, and she knew her casual tone hadn't fooled him. "For a few moments there I had the willies, but they didn't last." Sam flashed a crooked smile. "Your voice helps keep me steady."

"Samantha." Her name was little more than a groan. "You can't say stuff like that to me while we're working."

She had to laugh at his pained expression. "Okay, but it's true."

When she would've pulled away, he shook his head. "You don't have to finish your Lifeline rotation. I shouldn't have interfered in your request for a transfer. I'll talk to Jared on your behalf if you like."

"Reese." She turned toward him, looking him directly in the eye. "I'm fine. Seriously. As soon as we dropped our patient off, I realized how lucky he was to have Lifeline there for him. The closest trauma center was easily forty-five minutes by ground transport. He never would've lasted that long." Her expression clouded. "He still may not make it, but getting him here so quickly gives him a chance."

"Yes, that much is true. But the person to put their life on the line doesn't have to be you," Reese argued.

She studied him for a moment. Was he worried about a repeat of what had happened to Valerie? "I'm only here for a few months, Reese. When I graduate, I'll get a staff position in an emergency trauma center someplace. I won't be flying anymore."

Instead of relief, his expression turned even more somber. She didn't know what else to say to reassure him.

"I guess you'll just have to be my personal pilot," she teased lightly. "That way, you know I'll be in good hands."

Their pagers went off simultaneously before he could respond. Samantha looked at the message on the screen. "Car versus train, two victims in the car, both adults, but the woman is pregnant." Her heart squeezed in her chest. "Where's the peds crew?"

There was no answer as they ran toward the helicopter. Lifeline maintained two choppers just for this reason, although she knew full well the mother's life had to come first. Especially since they had no way of knowing the gestational age of the fetus.

"They're on their way to Children's Memorial with the transport. They'll respond if we give them the word," Reese informed her. "Come on, where's Andrew?"

"Right behind you, Ace." Andrew plunked his helmet on his head. "Ready to roll."

Samantha smiled as she jumped in behind you Andrew. Maybe working for some air medical transport company wouldn't be so bad if the crew was just like this. Certainly, she'd suffered worse rotations before.

She listened as Reese went through his preflight check,

then radioed the base. "Lifeline to base, come in. We're ready for takeoff."

"Roger, Lifeline, you're clear to go. Winds are coming out of the east."

"Roger."

Samantha listened as Reese communicated with the paramedic base. This time she didn't experience any of the previous preflight jitters as Reese took off.

The helicopter suddenly lurched hard to the right. If Sam hadn't been strapped in, she would've smashed up against her door.

Before she could cue her mic to ask Reese what happened, his voice came through her headset, calm and clear. "Mayday, Mayday. We're going down for an emergency landing."

12

Reese fought to keep the stick steady, sweat dripping down along the inside of his helmet, burning his eyes. *Come on, keep it level.* If he didn't hold the chopper level, the tip of his blades might hit something, sending them crashing. They'd be goners for sure.

The paramedic base rattled off commands in his ear, but he couldn't hear what they were saying through the thundering beat of his heart. He gripped the controls so hard he was surprised the handle didn't break in two. No matter how hard he tried to keep the chopper level, it kept lurching to the right. Something, a bird maybe, must've hit them, causing damage on the right side. They were only a few hundred feet up—all he needed to do was get back down onto the helipad.

Easier said than done. The wobbly motion of the helicopter was far from reassuring. He started his descent. The building was close, too close to the helipad for comfort. If he misjudged the lurching motion of the helicopter, they'd crash. Slowly lowering the chopper, he stared at the controls, fighting to keep the lopsided motion to a minimum. Finally, he landed, hard. He instantly cut the rotation of the blades just as one of the skids beneath the chopper gave away, sending them lurching sideways. The helicopter shuddered to a halt.

For a moment, he just sat there.

They'd made it down alive.

"Samantha? Andrew? Are you both all right?" Reese struggled to get out of his harness, the awkward angle of the chopper making it difficult.

"Reese? We're okay." Samantha's voice was reassuringly steady. "Can't get the door opened, though."

"Use your feet to kick out the window." Reese was forced to use the same maneuver to get out as well. He climbed from the chopper, thankful to see Samantha and Andrew were both already out and on the ground.

"What did you do to my chopper?" Mitch roared from the hangar doorway.

"Something hit us. Must've been a bird." Reese locked his knees to keep himself upright. But he couldn't hide his shaking hands as he reached toward Samantha. "Are you sure you're not hurt anywhere?"

"No, I'm fine." Samantha smiled and grasped his hands tightly. He wanted her in his arms, but she held him off. "Thanks for getting us down safely."

He almost hadn't, but he didn't think it was prudent to mention that fact. Slowly, he released her. The three of them headed inside the hangar. "We'll need to call base."

"Yeah, I want to know where the second helicopter is." Samantha barely glanced at him in her rush to get to the phone. "We need to respond to this call."

"What? Are you nuts?" Reese argued hotly. "We almost crashed."

Samantha ignored him. "Base, where's the second chopper? Tell them to hustle over to Lifeline. Our chopper is down, and we need to respond to this call. One of the crew members will need to switch with me."

"Samantha, you don't need to go." Reese tried to reason with her once she hung up the phone. "Someone else can help the victims."

"Let's help Mitch get the chopper off the helipad. The second one is on its way." Samantha wasn't listening.

He wanted to shake some sense into her. "Mitch has already hauled the busted chopper inside. But listen to me. You don't need to respond to this call."

"Yes, Reese, I do. There are two injured people out there who need me. One of them is pregnant. There isn't anyone else to go."

Before he could think of another argument, he heard the second chopper approach. Within minutes, the chopper landed on the helipad. Samantha pulled on her helmet and waited, ready to rush to the helicopter.

A guy he couldn't see clearly through the face shield of his helmet, jumped off, wordlessly agreeing to change places with Samantha.

In a heartbeat, Reese decided he wasn't letting her go alone. He rushed to the pilot's door and gestured his intention to ride along. Nate looked confused, but luckily the less senior pilot didn't argue.

Within moments, Reese was seated in the copilot's seat as Nate communicated to base his request to take off. Reese grabbed the armrests and held his breath, expecting the worst, as Nate lifted the chopper from the ground.

Jared wouldn't be happy with him, but he didn't care. Reese knew he was supposed to file a crash report on the hard landing, but as far as he was concerned, the report would have to wait.

If Samantha intended to go to the crash scene, he would go with her. Even if flying made his stomach bubble and roll like molten lava.

Samantha's palms were damp, and she wiped them on her flight suit as she took several steadying breaths. Flying so soon after the hard landing wasn't easy, but there wasn't another choice. If those people needed help, she intended to be there.

This was what she'd trained for. Saving lives.

She was grateful David, the peds resident, had agreed to switch places with her. With Shelly on board, they had one adult responder and one pediatric one, a good balance in her opinion. Her only regret was that Reese wasn't the pilot.

Would Reese fly again after their hard landing? She honestly didn't know. The crash that had taken his best friend and fiancée still haunted him. But he was an amazing pilot. She knew she and Andrew owed their lives to Reese's expertise in avoiding a serious crash.

She remained quiet while Nate communicated with the base regarding the location of the train versus car crash. Shelly didn't know anything about the hard landing, the paramedic base had only relayed the information of how Reese's chopper was down and unavailable to fly. Sam decided now wasn't the time to fill Shelly in on the gory details, not while they were in flight. Instead, she concentrated on the task at hand. There would be plenty of time to fall apart later.

"ETA two minutes." Nate's voice broke into her thoughts. "See that field over there? That's where I am bringing her down."

Shelly nodded, indicating she agreed with Nate's decision. Sam grabbed hold of her seat and held her breath as Nate settled the chopper on the ground with a jarring thud. In her humble opinion, Nate was not the pilot Reese was.

Samantha and Shelly jumped down, then went around the chopper to pull the gurney out from the hatch.

Sam surveyed the scene. The damage didn't look nearly as bad as it could've been considering a train was involved. The car was smashed in on the rear bumper of the driver's side, but it must have spun clear around as the front was wedged up against a tree. The paramedics on scene waved them forward.

"The driver is a male, he's the worst of the two. The woman is conscious, but she's trapped inside. She's also in active labor, crying that she feels the need to push. Has either of you delivered a baby?"

"I haven't helped deliver a baby since nursing school." Shelly's face was pale, and her hand hovered over her own slightly rounded abdomen. Belatedly, Samantha remembered hearing about Shelly's pregnancy.

"I have," Samantha admitted as she swallowed hard. "I did a two-month rotation in OB last year." She didn't add how delivering a baby in a controlled environment with the experts at hand was very different than managing the same task out in the field like this. "I'll take the mother."

"I'll examine the driver." Shelly didn't hide her relief.

"I'll give you a hand, Samantha." Reese's deep voice came from behind her.

She glanced over in shock to see him standing there, but there wasn't time to ask why he'd tagged along. "Fine. The paramedics can help Shelly." Shelly specialized in peds, but with the paramedics help, she would be able to handle the driver. "Reese, give me hand. We have to get her out of there or she'll be delivering that baby on her own."

Sam headed over to where a couple of firefighters were prying open the passenger door. Reese remained by her side.

"Almost got it," one of them said with a grunt. With one last pull, the door opened and fell to the ground.

Samantha crouched in the opening beside the sobbing woman. "I'm Dr. Kearn. Everything's okay. You need to help me now so we can save your baby." She sharpened her tone, trying to get through to the nearly hysterical woman. "How far apart are your contractions?"

"I don't know." The woman spoke between gasping sobs. Sam was glad she was trying to cooperate. The pregnant woman took a deep breath and then added, "Just before we crashed, they were five minutes apart. I don't have a watch, but they seem to be almost one right after the other."

Too close. That's exactly what Samantha had been afraid of. Any thoughts of loading her patient into the chopper and taking her directly to Trinity faded fast. "Are you hurt anywhere? Your neck? Your head? We need to get you out of this car."

"My head hurts a little, but nothing like these contractions." The woman gasped and cried out. "I was in such pain, Eddie was rushing me to the hospital. We thought we beat the train, but it clipped our bumper, sending us spinning into the tree." The woman's face contorted. "How is Eddie? Oh no, here's another one." She wailed as a contraction tightened her abdomen.

"Breathe through the pain, try to pant." Samantha wished she'd paid more attention during her OB rotation. When she'd assisted in delivering babies, the nurses had taken the role of coaches, instructing their patients how to breathe.

"Like this." Reese stepped up and demonstrated the technique, helping the woman breathe. Sam could barely hide her amazement. How did he know what to do?

"We need to turn her so I can examine her," Samantha told Reese in a low tone. "The baby is close."

"Got it."

Between them, they got the woman turned in the seat enough that Sam could kneel on the icy ground in front of the passenger door to examine her patient. Sure enough, there was a round bulge where the baby's head was crowning.

There wasn't time to think. "All right, the next time you feel a contraction, I want you to push."

"Are you sure?" Reese's eyebrows rose as if he were nervous.

"Yes, I'm sure. This baby isn't going to wait much longer." Sam tried to smile reassuringly at the woman. There weren't stirrups to use, so she hooked one of her patient's legs over her own shoulder and propped the other one on the rail of the paramedic's gurney. Without a fetal monitor, she could only hope and pray that the baby was okay.

"I feel one coming." The woman tried to struggle into a sitting position.

"Reese, help her sit up, will you?"

He quickly obeyed, doing his best to anchor the patient's leg on the rail of the gurney before crawling in beside her, putting his hand beneath her back.

"Ow, it hurts," she whimpered.

"I know, but you need to push. Come on, push hard." Samantha kept her hand over the top of the baby's head as the woman pushed. She heard Reese speaking to the woman in his low, husky voice, reassuring her about how great she was doing. Slowly, the head and face emerged. Sam gently guided the birth, turning the baby's head to the side and using her index finger to make sure the umbilical cord wasn't wrapped around the neck.

Thankfully, she couldn't feel the cord. "Now push again. The baby is almost out. We only need to get past the shoulders. Come on, push." Samantha was grateful for Reese's help as he gave words of encouragement through the woman's sobs while she pushed.

Tiny shoulders emerged from the birth canal, and the rest of the baby quickly followed. She felt Reese's awed gaze on hers as Samantha held the tiny, slippery infant. She quickly used the portable suction from their equipment pack to clear the baby's nose and mouth.

She did a quick mental Apgar score, estimating it to be in the six to seven range. As soon as she'd suctioned the baby's mouth, the infant began to cry. Relief washed over her, and sudden tears made her blink. "A boy. You have a beautiful baby boy."

"A boy!" The woman was sobbing in earnest now, but the radiant happiness on her features reassured Sam that these were tears of joy. "Is he all right? Please tell me he's going to be all right."

"He's fine. Listen to him cry," Reese said with a relieved smile. "He sounds like a healthy boy."

Samantha used the blanket from the gurney to wrap around the infant, then placed the baby in the mother's arms before tending to the umbilical cord. Using string from a sterile suture pack, she tied off the cord and then cut it with bandage scissors. The scissors weren't sterile but clean enough, she hoped.

Birth was such a miracle. For long moments, she and

Reese could only gaze at the mother holding her baby. When Reese's eyes, full of wonder, met hers, she had to fight another surge of tears. The expression in Reese's gaze mirrored her thoughts. Thank heavens, they'd gotten there when they had. Paramedics probably would've done fine, but her expertise, as little as it was, hadn't hurt.

After the placenta was delivered, she asked Reese for help in placing the woman on the gurney.

"How in the world did you know what to do?" She glanced at him with appreciation as she made sure the mother and baby were comfortable. "Have you assisted with deliveries before?"

"Sort of. I had to step in and help out my sister when she gave birth to my nephew, Aiden, because her husband was overseas and couldn't get back." The tips of Reese's ears burned bright red. "Breathing was the only thing I remember, the rest was a big blur. There are some things a brother shouldn't watch."

Samantha laughed. "Well, you helped tremendously. I'm so relieved they're both doing fine." With a guilty start, she remembered their other patient. She turned toward the opposite side of the car. "Have you heard anything about the driver?"

"No."

"Stay here." Samantha jogged over to where the driver was stretched out on the grass in the field. She kneeled beside Shelly and the paramedic. "How is he?"

"He's not doing well." Shelly glanced up with a frown. "Heavy bleeding internally, I suspect. We can't get volume into him fast enough."

Of the two, the driver needed to get to the hospital the fastest. Sam turned to the paramedic helping Shelly. "You guys need to take mom and baby to Trinity by ambulance. Reese? We need to take the driver in the chopper."

"Gotcha." The paramedic stood and headed back to where mother and baby were waiting. He quickly wheeled the gurney to the nearest waiting ambulance.

Samantha returned to the driver. Reese came to help them lift the male patient onto the Lifeline gurney. "Let's get airborne. We can pump fluids into him en route. The only thing that will help him now is getting to the OR."

With help from Reese's strong muscles, they hauled their patient through the field into the waiting chopper. When they were finished storing their patient through the rear hatch, Reese climbed in beside Nate. Sam instructed Shelly to keep pumping fluids and blood into their patient while they flew to Trinity. She couldn't imagine losing the woman's husband, Eddie.

He deserved to see his newborn son.

"Hang on, Eddie," she whispered, squeezing the unit of blood with her gloved hands to make it go faster. "You have a son who needs you. Hang on."

"His blood pressure is only seventy systolic," Shelly informed her.

"Keep the fluids going wide open," Sam instructed. "Has all of our blood already been given?"

"Third unit of O Neg infusing now. It's our last unit of blood."

Sam's stomach knotted with tension. They couldn't lose Eddie. They just couldn't.

"ETA four minutes," Nate informed them.

The news brightened her spirits. It may just be enough time. "Reese? Call Trinity and request they have an OR trauma team ready to go."

"Roger."

She listened, keeping an eye on Eddie's blood pressure as Reese did as she asked. By the time Nate landed, the ED crew was waiting for them. Within moments, they rushed Eddie into the operating room where the trauma surgical team was on standby, ready to explore the patient's abdomen to find the source of the bleeding.

Samantha's shoulders slumped as the doors shut behind them. There was nothing more to do. Eddie's life was in good hands now. If the trauma surgeons at Trinity Medical Center couldn't save him, no one could.

"Hey, I heard you delivered a baby boy." Shelly smiled, her hand once again hovering over her abdomen. "I'm so glad you were there. I don't think I could've delivered a baby."

Sam tried to smile. "Let's just hope he has a chance to know his dad."

"I know." Shelly's expression clouded, and Sam wondered if she was thinking of the risks of her own career.

Sam knew they couldn't save all their patients, no one could. Still, she couldn't imagine how that poor wife would feel to know she had lost her husband in the process of gaining a son.

Up on the helipad, Nate and Reese waited to take them back to Lifeline. Samantha felt drained, too exhausted to feel nervous about flying. Shelly also remained quiet as they returned to Lifeline's hangar.

Jared was waiting for them on the helipad when they landed. By the furrows creasing his brow, she could tell he was not happy.

Nate shut down the engine. Everyone jumped out of the chopper. Shelly headed straight for her husband, giving him a big hug. Jared returned the gesture, pressing a kiss to the top of his wife's head, but his face remained grim.

"What's up?" Nate wanted to know.

"Jared?" Reese approached more slowly. "I know I need to do a crash report. I'll do it right now."

"A crash report?" Shelly echoed. "What are you talking about? What happened?"

"A bird or something struck the chopper just as we were taking off," Sam informed her. "Reese had to bring us down in an emergency landing."

"Oh my goodness." Shelley looked horrified. "I've read about others suffering hard landings, but I've never experienced one."

Sam grimaced. She wouldn't recommend the experience. "We were fine, thanks to Reese, but you should see the chopper. It's in pretty bad shape."

"I'm not concerned about the crash report." Jared finally spoke, his words slow and deliberate as his gaze encompassed all of them. "But you need to know, the chopper wasn't struck by a bird. Mitch found a bullet hole in the right side of the engine. Someone took a shot at you."

A wave of nausea washed over her. "Someone shot at us? You mean, on purpose?" She glanced at Reese, afraid to verbalize her thoughts out loud.

Because the only person she could imagine doing such a terrible thing was Dennis.

13

Samantha stared in horror at the round bullet hole Mitch obligingly showed her in the engine, trying to assimilate what the evidence so glaringly pointed out.

Had Dennis really done this? Could he have gone that far over the deep end?

Maybe there wasn't any hard evidence pointing to Dennis as the culprit, but who else could it be? It wasn't as if Lifeline made a lot of enemies that the bullet would be a random act of some disgruntled customer. In the middle of February, in the heart of the city, there was no chance of a freak hunting accident.

This must have been an intentional act.

The sick feeling in her stomach told her it was Dennis. He never owned a gun when they were together, but that didn't mean he didn't have one now. The smashed battery and the brick through her window already proved he was capable of violence. But this was worse. Much worse.

He'd almost killed the entire crew.

Think. She needed to think. "Have you notified the police?"

"Yes. I've already given them a statement." Jared nodded toward the office. "They're waiting for both of you."

Reese fell into step beside her, but his dark gaze was difficult to read.

This entire mess was her fault, and she knew it. She'd caused Reese to be relive his worst nightmare. They'd almost crashed—had, in fact, suffered a hard landing. Reese must've thought he was about to end up like Valerie a dozen times. Sam should've tried much harder to convince Jared to find a replacement for her. Her request for reassignment had been token at best. With Brandon's evidence, she'd honestly thought her problems with Dennis were over.

Obviously not.

"Have they arrested Dennis yet?" she asked as she and Reese made their way through the hangar toward Jared's office.

Jared shook his head. "No, and I gave them a piece of my mind about that. How difficult can it be for the entire Milwaukee Police Department to find one man?"

Samantha held her tongue. Dennis had managed to slip through the fingers of the police for a long time. Personally, she had more faith in Brandon Rafter's chances of bringing him in.

The door of Jared's office was open, and there were two uniformed police officers seated inside. They stood when she and Reese entered.

Reese remained close to her, giving her a sense of security. He had every right to be angry with her, but she knew his protective instincts well enough to know he'd stick with her until Dennis was taken into custody. Guilt churned in her belly. Thanks to her, Reese had almost been killed. Andrew, too. The thought made her sick.

"This is Dr. Samantha Kearn." Jared introduced her to the officers. "We have good reason to suspect her ex-husband is the one who fired at the helicopter."

Sam recognized one of the officers as the same guy who'd come to investigate after the brick had been hurled through her bedroom window. She nodded at him in greeting.

"Dr. Kearn, we have a few questions for you." The older of the two men gestured toward a vacant seat. "Please sit down."

Because the trembling in her knees was so bad, she gratefully sat and folded her hands in her lap. "What do you need?"

"When was the last time you saw your ex-husband?" he wanted to know.

Sam tempered a flare of impatience. "I haven't actually seen him at all." She thought back over the flower delivery, the note under her door, and the brick through her window. After all of that, why would they think she'd spoken to him?

Wait a minute. She *had* seen Dennis. Abruptly, she straightened in her seat. In the lobby of Trinity Medical Center, she'd witnessed the brief meeting between Dennis and her boss, Dr. Ben Harris.

"Wait, that's not true," Sam admitted slowly. "I did see Dennis, the other day, in the lobby at Trinity Medical Center."

"When?" Reese asked sharply.

She nearly winced. She hadn't intended to keep this a big secret. "The day I went to do Andrew's follow-up visits. I saw Dennis. He was dressed in a very nice suit, and he was shaking hands with Dr. Harris."

"Ben Harris? The medical director of Trinity's emergency department?" Jared asked.

"Yes. I was shocked when I saw them together, especially because, technically, Dr. Harris is my boss." She turned toward the officers. "Dennis is a pharmaceutical sales rep. I assumed he was meeting with Dr. Harris on business."

"Did Markowitz see you?" Reese asked, his voice was low, vibrating with anger.

"I don't know." She remembered her quick dash across the lobby, trying to hide her face in the collar of her Lifeline jacket. "We'd just got a call for a transfer, so I bolted through the front door without looking back."

The older officer turned toward Jared. "Where exactly is Dr. Harris's office?"

Jared gestured through the small window. In the medical staff office building, you can see the white building right there." The office building was adjacent to Trinity Medical Center for the convenience of the physicians.

"We need to speak with him," the younger officer said.

"I'm coming with you." Sam quickly stood. She wanted to know for herself, too. Had she made things worse by not telling her boss the entire truth about Dennis? She couldn't imagine Dennis was setting up a meeting with Ben Harris, giving him a sob story of the aggrieved ex-husband trying to reconcile with his wife. It seemed so farfetched. Ben certainly knew about her divorce, if not the gory details.

Reese stayed with her as they all walked over to the medical staff office building. Jared led the way to the seventh floor where all the emergency department staff physicians' offices were located.

"Grace, tell Dr. Harris we need to see him," Jared told the medical staff secretary seated in the outer office. "It's important."

"I would, Dr. O'Connor, but Dr. Harris is in Chicago, attending a trauma lecture." Grace's wide eyes flickered between the group, noting with interest the police officers standing behind Sam. "I can contact him, if needed."

"Go ahead. Or maybe you can help us." Jared stepped closer. "Do you know why Dr. Harris met with Dennis Markowitz?"

"Markowitz. The name rings a bell." Grace went to work on the computer. "Oh, yes. I remember setting this meeting up. Dennis Markowitz requested a meeting with Dr. Harris regarding a business matter." She peered at them over the top of her glasses and shrugged. "I don't know anything more detailed, I'm afraid."

"Did Dr. Harris often meet with sales reps?" Samantha asked.

Grace wrinkled her nose with distaste. "No, not often."

"Get Harris on the line," Jared instructed. "And can you let us into his office?"

"Sure." Grace hastily stood, grabbed a set of keys off her desk, and led the way down the hall. "Dr. Harris's office is the last one here, in the corner."

She opened the door and gasped, taking a step back when a cold blast of air hit. "Good heavens! It's so cold. Why, the window is open."

Samantha edged inside, the sick feeling in her stomach twisting like a snake trying to get loose. The window was indeed open, not much, but enough to show someone had been in there. But that wasn't what robbed her of speech. No, the worst part was that the fact that her boss's office directly overlooked Lifeline's helipad.

She barely listened as the questions started all over again.

"What time did you get in this morning?" the officers asked Grace. "How long has Dr. Ben Harris been gone?"

"He left yesterday, no, the day before." The poor woman wrung her hands in distress. "I came in at the usual time, eight thirty this morning."

"We were in flight by zero seven thirty," Reese told the officers. "The shot came within minutes after takeoff."

"How did Markowitz get in? Was the office locked this morning?"

Grace shook her head miserably. "Not the main office area. The attending physician on duty in the ED usually comes up early, prior to the start of their shift. They open the general office area, drop off their stuff, then go down to work. The individual offices are locked, though," she added helpfully.

"He must've gotten in somehow." Jared sounded distinctly annoyed. "We need to find him before he succeeds in doing something far worse."

The officers agreed, and more assistance was requested to record the potential crime scene. From what Sam could tell, Dennis hadn't left any evidence other than the open window.

Reese pulled Sam and Jared aside. "We need to make some decisions about future flights. Maybe we should remain grounded until he's caught."

Samantha sucked in a quick breath. The idea of refusing calls went against her nature. "Do you think that's necessary? He isn't here now. He's too smart to hang around. I'm sure he's long gone."

"Maybe, but we don't know where he is," Reese argued.

"I have to agree." Jared frowned. "All we can do is add pressure to get the police to capture him more quickly."

"I think it would be best to let me resign." Samantha

couldn't stand to be the cause of more grief. "The repairs on the chopper will take a while anyway. You won't need two crews."

"I won't accept your resignation," Jared said firmly. "But I agree you should remain grounded, at least until Markowitz is caught."

Sam didn't like it and vowed to find a way to resign. Arguing with Jared wasn't going to help. She risked a glance at Reese. "What about Reese? It's possible Dennis saw us together." Her cheeks flamed, but she held her head up high. She wasn't ashamed of anything she'd done. Kissing Reese wasn't a crime. Yet if Dennis had seen them...

She knew she should've stayed away from Reese, but she hadn't listened to the voice of reason. Instead, her desire to spend time with Reese had nearly killed them all.

"Dennis is possessive and controlling." She took a deep breath and let it out slowly. She couldn't bear to look at Reese. "I'm not sure, but I think his violence may have escalated because he saw us together down at the lakefront."

The knowledge was sobering. If she hadn't agreed to spend the day with Reese, it was possible none of this would have happened.

REESE MUTTERED A CURSE, a word he hadn't used since his Air Force days. He should have known something like this would happen. By trying to protect Samantha, he'd made things worse.

No, he hadn't made things worse by protecting her, but because he hadn't been able to stay away from her. He'd crossed the line of friendship and, as a result, sent Markowitz into a frenzy.

He forced himself to remain calm. "I'll agree to being grounded, but first I need to take a brief trip in the air." Flying alongside Nate as a copilot wasn't quite the same as flying himself. Reese knew if he didn't get up with his hand on the stick soon, he'd lose his nerve.

Jared must've understood because he nodded. "Fine. Let's head back to Lifeline."

They made their way to the front part of the office. Grace waved at them, phone up to her ear. "Wait. Dr. O'Connor? I have Dr. Harris on the line."

Samantha put a hand on Jared's arm. "Let me speak to him."

Jared hesitated, then gestured for her to go ahead.

Reese listened intently to her one-sided conversation.

"Ben? It's Samantha Kearn. I'm sorry to bother you, but I need to understand why you met with Dennis Markowitz the other day?" She fell silent, the corner of her mouth turned down in a frown. "I see. I never thought he'd ask your personal advice about our divorce. I'm sorry. I should have told you I have a restraining order against him." Another pause, then she said, "I've tried to give my resignation to Dr. O'Connor, but he won't accept it. Yes, I'll have him call you when you return. Thanks, Ben." She hung up the phone.

"Markowitz actually contacted your boss for advice on getting you back?" Reese couldn't believe what he'd heard.

Sam nodded. "It's my fault. I should've told Ben the truth upfront, but I was too embarrassed."

"About what?" Reese was genuinely confused.

She ducked her head. "I'm training to be a physician. I felt foolish for falling for someone like Dennis. For allowing myself to get involved with a control freak and emotional abuser."

"That's not your fault." Reese wanted to draw her close, to provide reassurance. But with Jared right there, he held off.

"Easy to say, not so easy to believe."

He let it go. He wondered if she'd convinced her boss to find a replacement for her at Lifeline. On one hand, he wanted Samantha out of danger. The near miss this morning still rattled his bones. But on the other hand, the idea of losing Samantha was unthinkable.

Yet, once she left Lifeline and Markowitz was no longer a threat, she wouldn't need him anymore. He tried not to dwell on his own selfishness.

Back at Lifeline, Reese completed the rest of the paperwork surrounding the hard landing. The FAA would need to talk to him as well, he knew. Since the peds crew was out on a call, he didn't have the opportunity to take a chopper up, although they were expected back soon.

He glanced down at his trembling hands, hoping he could still fly. It wouldn't be easy. Riding shotgun with Nate had been difficult enough.

Samantha poked her head into the debriefing room. "I just called to check on our patients. Mom and baby are doing great. Eddie made it through surgery, but he's still in critical condition."

More proof that there were no guarantees. It dawned on Reese that if he married someday, his child could grow up without a father, too. With an effort, he pushed his morbid thoughts aside.

"I'm ready to head home," Samantha told him.

"I'll come with you." He shoved his report aside. Since they were both grounded, there was no reason to stick around.

She shrugged, avoiding his gaze. "If you want, but I have my car here."

He remembered her stubborn insistence on driving separate vehicles. "I can drive you home." Reese couldn't bear to let her out of his sight. Not while Markowitz was still on the loose.

"I don't want to leave my car here. Remember what happened last time?" Samantha's mouth was set in the familiar stubborn line. "You can follow me, if that makes you feel better."

It didn't, but since their apartment complex was only a few miles away, he figured it would have to do. "Fine, I'll follow you. But we're going to my place."

Samantha's expression was troubled. He expected an argument, but she nodded. "I guess we should talk."

Talk? His gut clenched. Was this when she'd give him the brush-off? *Thanks, it was fun, but since you almost got me killed, I think it's better if we don't see each other anymore?*

With a grimace, he knew he couldn't blame her. Silently he grabbed his coat, then held hers out for her, before heading outside.

The day was cloudy and cold. He waited until Samantha was safe inside her car with the engine running before heading to his. He'd purposefully parked several spots away so it wouldn't be too obvious that they'd arrived together.

He turned the key in the ignition, but his car wouldn't start. With a frown, he tried again. Was it possible his battery was dead? It wasn't an old car. His lights turned off automatically, and all his doors were closed.

The image of Samantha's hammer-smashed battery came to mind. He popped the hood and slid out from behind the wheel. He waved at Samantha, indicating she should come over.

Instead, she looked at him, a strange expression in her eyes. She waved, then slowly drove away.

"Wait!" He started after her. The silhouette of a second head appeared in the back window of her ancient Oldsmobile, and his heart squeezed painfully.

Someone was in the car with her. *Markowitz.*

Reese didn't stop to think. He ran inside Lifeline and shouted at Jared. "Call nine-one-one. Markowitz is in the back seat of Samantha's car."

Without waiting for response, he hurried through the building to the hangar, then outside to the helipad. The second chopper had just landed. Impatiently, he grabbed his helmet and gestured for Nate to get out.

Nate shut the engine down and jumped out. Reese snatched the keys from his hand. "Hey, what are you doing?" Nate protested.

"I'm going up. Markowitz has Samantha." He jumped into the pilot seat and started the engine. Communicating with the paramedic base wasted precious seconds, but he couldn't afford to lift off without them knowing. For all he knew, they could accept a transfer from another helicopter transport company without realizing he was up there.

"Paramedic base, this is Lifeline. I'm taking off." He buckled his harness with a snap. "I also need you to patch me through to the police."

"Roger, Lifeline, but where are you going?" The dispatcher sounded confused. "We aren't aware of a call."

"Patch me through to the police," Reese repeated. For a nanosecond he hesitated, then took a breath, pushed the stick forward, and lifted the chopper airborne. Banking left, he circled the area over the Lifeline parking lot and scanned the road below, searching for Samantha's car.

His heart hammered in his chest when he didn't see the familiar Oldsmobile. Then his gaze picked out a large burgundy-colored vehicle just a couple of miles away from the parking lot. The car seemed to be moving deliberately slower than the rest of the traffic, heading away from the city on a small highway rather than the interstate. There were other cars, but Samantha's older model vehicle had a bulky frame that stood out from the rest.

"Found you," he whispered in satisfaction. "Base, do you have the police yet? I'm following Dr. Samantha Kearn's vehicle west on Highway Twenty. Dennis Markowitz is the suspect inside."

"You're using the helicopter to follow someone?" The dispatcher's voice rose in alarm. "That's not allowed. We don't have that as part of the flight plan."

Reese gnashed his teeth. "All the more reason to put me through to the police. Now!" They could call up the entire National Guard as far as he was concerned. Samantha was in trouble. He didn't care how help arrived.

"All right, I hear you." The dispatcher paused, then came back on the radio. "Go ahead, the police are on the same frequency. Officer, you're on." The dispatcher finally turned the mic over to the police.

"You have the suspect in sight? What's the make of the vehicle?" the officer wanted to know.

"Burgundy Oldsmobile, heading west on Highway Twenty." Reese hovered over Samantha's car, wishing he could do more. "I don't know the license plate number. It's too far away for me to read."

"And you're certain Markowitz is inside?" There was a hint of uncertainty in the officer's tone.

There was no doubt in Reese's mind that he'd seen two figures in the car. Since Samantha had gone to her car alone, he figured Markowitz must've been hiding in the back seat. But, was Reese sure enough to stake her life on it? "Yes, I'm certain."

"When they get out of the city, we'll set up a roadblock," the officer informed him. "Keep the car in sight."

"I will." There was no way he'd lose her now.

The palms of his hands were sweaty on the stick, but Reese couldn't afford the luxury of being nervous. He had to fly high enough to avoid treacherous power lines at the same time making sure he wasn't so high he lost Samantha.

He absolutely refused to lose her ever again.

Up ahead, he could see a long stretch of highway, relatively free of traffic. Sure enough, there were several police cars setting up the promised roadblock.

"Hang on, Samantha," he prayed. With a wide sweeping curve, he came back around, keeping the burgundy car in sight. "Officer, I see the roadblock. The suspect's car is headed directly toward it."

"Ten-four. We have a sharpshooter in position to take out the vehicle's tires," the officer replied.

"What?" Reese shouted, his hands slipped on the stick. He quickly straightened the chopper. "What if she crashes?"

"We need to get the car off the road. I've been told there's a possibility the suspect has weapons in his possession."

He didn't doubt Markowitz had the gun he'd used to shoot down his chopper, so Reese swallowed his protest. Samantha was cool under pressure, he'd seen her in action more than once. She'd saved countless lives while flying thousands of feet in the air. She wouldn't crash. She'd be fine.

Dear God, please let her be fine.

As if watching a movie in slow motion, he saw her vehicle slow dramatically, then swerve wildly on the road when the tire blew out. He held his breath until the car came to a wobbly stop, then desperately sought a close place to land.

He decided the stretch of highway that the cops conveniently blocked off would have to do. Without sparing more than a passing thought to the last time he landed, Reese lowered the chopper down onto the concrete surface.

After shutting down the engine, he jumped out. Samantha's car was just thirty yards away. He heard cops shouting at him, but he didn't listen.

Then he saw her. He stopped abruptly in his tracks. Samantha's car door opened, and she emerged from inside with Markowitz right behind her.

He held a knife to her throat.

14

Samantha saw Reese, wanted to run straight toward him, but she didn't dare breathe when Dennis whispered, "You didn't come back to me. Why not? Because of lover-boy over there?"

Dear heaven, she didn't know what to do. Dennis seemed beyond reason. Reese was so close, yet she didn't dare acknowledge him for fear Dennis would turn his wrath on him.

Stall. She needed more time.

"We're surrounded," she began, but when the knife pressed closer, she clamped her mouth shut. For support, she held onto the arm he'd wrapped around her neck as he forced her to walk forward. He wouldn't listen to reason anyway. Bile rose in her throat, threatening to choke her. The entire time he'd been in the car, he kept trying to convince her everything was her fault.

Months ago, she may have believed him. It was her fault she married him, but that was the extent of it. Seeing Dennis now, she realized she was not in charge of his actions.

No one was but him. It was time he faced the truth.

"Tell them you made a mistake," he hissed in her ear. Slowly, he turned her in a circle so everyone could see the knife he held to her throat. "Tell them you're my wife and your place is at home with me. Tell them!"

Sam bit back a cry, her grip on his arm slipping when his hand tightened.

"Tell them this is all your fault. You never should've left me, Sammie. You never should have left."

She shivered, his whispered voice haunting her, flooding her with memories of the past. How many times had she listened to similar taunts? The familiar lethargy seeped through her pores, sapping her will to fight. She knew Dennis would rather kill her than give up to the police.

Maybe that was for the best. It would end, right here, right now.

Her gaze settled on Reese standing statue still while he stared at her, his gaze imploring her to hang on. Abruptly, she knew Reese would risk his life for her.

The idea snapped the invisible hold Dennis wielded. Reese had faced his fears, flying the helicopter to find her. She deserved a normal life, and no way was she going to let Dennis the Menace control her for another second.

She sent Reese a warning glance, trying without words to tell him what she was about to do. She subtly tightened her grasp on Dennis's arm, then stomped on his foot at the same time pushing with all her strength against his arm. Dennis wasn't used to her fighting back. For a second, he yelped in pain and loosened his grip, just enough so she could tear herself free.

"No," he cried. "You're mine, Sammie. You're mine!"

Ignoring his outburst, she ran straight toward Reese, who simultaneously sprinted toward her. He caught her in his arms and held her close. There was a stampede of movement behind her, shouts from several officers, and just that quickly, Dennis was facedown on the ground, being handcuffed and placed under arrest.

"You're safe, Samantha. Thank God above, you're safe," Reese murmured against her hair.

She buried her face in his shoulder, breathed in his scent, and sobbed. She knew, without looking, that the police had taken custody of Dennis. He was probably still trying to blame everything on her, but this time they wouldn't listen.

He would be held accountable for his actions.

It was finally over.

REESE WAS glad Samantha didn't need to spend too much time with the police. They'd found a rifle in the back seat of her car and had seized the weapon, suspecting it was the one used to shoot at the chopper. Apparently, it had been too long and awkward to use in controlling Samantha, so Dennis had pulled out a knife.

Reese held onto Samantha's hand, unwilling to let her go as she finished her statement. When she was ready to leave, he steered her toward the helicopter he'd left sitting in the middle of the road.

"I couldn't believe it when I watched you land this thing," Samantha confessed.

"Yeah." Reese knew the memory of what had nearly happened would stay with him forever. Reluctantly he released her hand and opened the chopper door. "I lost ten years off my life when I saw him through the back window of your car. I'm sorry, Samantha."

She raised a brow, then plunked her helmet on her head. "Sorry for what? I insisted on driving separately, if you recall. And now that it's all over, I'm glad. Dennis is finally in custody. He can't control me anymore."

Reese fell silent as he put his helmet on, then gestured for her to get into the front seat. He was very glad her ex couldn't torment her ever again, but at the same time, his usefulness was over.

She didn't need his protection anymore.

In a few more months, Samantha would graduate from her emergency medicine residency and take her boards. He had no doubt she'd pass, then she'd head out to San Diego, three thousand miles from Wisconsin.

His heart squeezed painfully in his chest. Ignoring the sense of loss, he communicated with the paramedic base, explaining that he was about to take off and return to Lifeline. He imagined the dispatcher was dying to know what had happened, but she simply gave him the go-ahead.

"Everything is so beautiful from up here." Samantha gazed out the window.

He didn't comment but silently agreed. He could appreciate how the chopper had helped save Samantha from harm. Safety would always be his top concern, but his team approach would help ensure that would always be the case for the rest of the crew.

It was time he stopped dwelling on the "what ifs" of the past and focus his attention on the future.

Back at Lifeline, they found Jared pacing the length of the hangar.

"Jarvis! What kind of stunt was that?"

Reese straightened his spine but refused to apologize. "I understand you're angry, Jared. But Samantha's life was in danger."

Jared blew out a long breath. "I'm glad you're okay, Samantha," he told her before turning back to Reese. "But you are not a cop. What were you thinking?"

"I was thinking about Samantha." Reese stood his ground. If Jared wanted to turn him over to the authorities, so be it. He had taken the helicopter to use in a non-FAA approved fashion. "I understood the risk and would take it again if need be."

Samantha frowned and reached out to place a hand on Jared's arm. "What risks? Jared, Dennis was hiding in the back seat of my car. He must have made a spare set of keys while we were still married. Reese was only trying to look out for me."

"I know." Jared reached up and yanked on his hair with both hands as if to pull the strands right out of his head. "This place is driving me nuts. I have a Board of Directors to answer to. I'll give you this one, Jarvis. We'll write this trip off as your way of getting back in the air after the forced landing. But don't try this sort of stunt again."

"I'm not planning to," Reese agreed.

Samantha tugged on Jared's arm. "Do you have a minute? I need to talk to you about something."

"Sure." Resigned, Jared's anger deflated into a puff of smoke. He spun on his heel and headed toward his office. Samantha and Reese followed.

Samantha sent him a questioning look. "I'm fine, Reese. You don't need to stay glued to my side."

The dread in his gut swirled like aviation fuel mixing with water. "Oh. I didn't realize you needed to talk to Jared in private." He couldn't prevent his tone from sounding stiff, formal.

Her expression softened. "It's nothing like that. You can come if you'd like."

He wasn't reassured but couldn't bring himself to leave. In Jared's office, she went straight to the point. "I need a favor. I've decided not to continue in emergency medicine after I graduate."

What? Reese stared at her. She loved her job. Her ex was finally out of the picture. What was she talking about?

"What do you need from me?" Jared asked, his forehead furrowed with concern.

"I need a recommendation for placement in the critical care fellowship program." She spoke in a rush. "They have one at Trinity Medical Center. I've decided I don't like handing over the care of my patients to the critical care team. I need to take a more active role in making them well."

Jared's eyebrows rose in surprise. "You'll probably need an extra year of medical residency to qualify," he warned her. "Plus, the fellowship is for three years. On the other hand, they have open positions to fill. You stand a good chance of landing one here."

"I know." Samantha's face practically glowed. "I spend too much time wondering about how my patients are doing. And this is probably something I should have done a long time ago."

Reese couldn't believe what he was hearing. He should have been elated by her news, but he couldn't shake the inward feeling of alarm. If Samantha was staying in Milwaukee, he had a chance at a real relationship. Possible future. Marriage. The home. Children.

All the things he once planned with Valerie.

He swallowed hard. Now that the coast was clear, he hesitated on the edge of the cliff, unable to jump. What if he committed himself to Samantha, only to lose her anyway?

"Reese?" Samantha waved a hand in front of his eyes,

her voice full concern. "Are you all right? Maybe you should sit down."

"I'm fine." His voice was muffled as if he were talking through the thickness of his helmet. He cleared his throat and tried again. "What about San Diego?"

Her eyes widened in surprise. "San Diego?"

"Yeah. Your family lives there." He felt foolish but pressed on. "I overheard you talking to Jared about moving back home once you graduated."

"I didn't realize you knew about that." Samantha tilted her head quizzically, then shrugged her shoulder. "That was the old me talking. The one who used to try to run from Dennis. But I don't want to leave." She smiled. "I want to stay here, in Milwaukee."

Panic swished and sloshed like a half empty rain barrel in his chest. "You do?"

Her questioning gaze turned into a wounded one, and he knew his reaction wasn't what she'd hoped to hear. Still, she squared her shoulders and glanced away. "Yes, I do. I have friends here. I don't want to leave."

Reese fell silent. Samantha had bravely fought against Markowitz and won. Did he possess the same bravery to fight against the ghosts in his past?

To love again, without any guarantee of forever?

SAMANTHA STOOD in front of her closet, trying to decide what to wear. Jared had called a few hours earlier, asking her to attend the Children's Memorial Hospital fundraiser ball in his place because Shelly was sick. Samantha had agreed to go, although she wasn't in the mood to celebrate.

She hadn't seen Reese in days since they'd both been

grounded. Now that Dennis wasn't a threat, she suspected their schedules wouldn't match.

Not that it should matter either way. She needed to finish these last few months at Lifeline. Going into critical care was the right decision for her career. She probably would've made the switch sooner if she'd been thinking clearly. So what if her goal of becoming a physician was put off for another couple of years? She had the rest of her life.

A life that obviously didn't include Reese. The back of her eyes ached with the effort to hold back tears. He'd overheard her plan to move to San Diego after graduation. Clearly, he'd kissed her, grown close to her while thinking the relationship was temporary.

No surprise. She always knew he was still hung up on Valerie.

She should've understood. Reese wasn't the type of a guy to fall in love easily. Still, she'd hoped . . .

Never mind. She would be happy that Dennis was in jail and that she had her life back. Ridiculous to want more.

She pulled out the only real formal dress she owned, a long red velvet dress that clung to her figure with a slit that showed off her legs when she walked. An eye-catching dress, but one she'd wear without enthusiasm.

She quickly put on a little makeup and fluffed her hair, leaving it down to wave around her shoulders. A glance at her watch made her grab a wool shoulder wrap and head for the door.

Jared had mentioned something about a car picking her up, but she hadn't expected to see a stretch black limo parked outside her modest apartment building. When she stepped outside, a driver, dressed sharply in black, jumped out to open the door for her.

"Thank you." She slid into the seat and glanced around

inside. She didn't mind being spoiled, but somehow her sense of loneliness only increased sitting in the expansive back seat. Alone. A limo ride was something to be shared.

Her heart ached, wishing Reese could love her, but she'd been down that road before. Dennis hadn't loved her either. He had been obsessed with controlling her and had been jealous of her success in a career he'd failed in, but he hadn't loved her.

She pushed thoughts of Reese aside and tried to enjoy her brief foray in luxury.

The limo driver let her out in front of the Milwaukee Art Museum, which overlooked Lake Michigan in downtown Milwaukee. The white structure was unique, inside and out. Samantha clutched her wrap and gazed around the expanse of glass and marble foyer.

A discrete host took her wrap when she introduced herself, telling him she was representing Dr. Jared O'Connor from Lifeline Air Rescue.

"We are pleased to have you here, Dr. Kearn. Can I get you something to drink?"

"A glass of Chardonnay, thank you."

Samantha gazed around the room, searching for a familiar face. When she didn't find anyone she knew, she took a sip of her wine and escaped the crowd by heading down the core door to a special Vincent van Gogh exhibit.

The impressive paintings on the walls reflected her pensive mood. How long since she'd taken the time to appreciate art? She paused before a breathtaking scenic painting, *The Bridge at Trinquetaille*.

"Nice, but not nearly as beautiful as you."

Samantha slowly turned toward the familiar husky male voice behind her.

"Hello, Reese." She could barely get the greeting past the

constriction in her throat. He was incredibly handsome in a tux, seemingly at home in formalwear as he was in his navy blue flight suit. "I didn't expect to see you here."

"Jared asked me to come in his place. He must've asked you, too."

"Yes." She raised a brow. "You didn't get a limo ride, though."

He tucked his hands in his pockets. "Maybe you'll share with me on the ride home."

She hesitated, then nodded, already missing the easy companionship she shared with him during their flights. The awkwardness between them now was painful. "Of course."

"I'd like to talk to you for a moment. Have a seat." She did as he asked, but the somber expression on his face made her heart squeeze painfully. Did Reese feel he needed to give her the brush-off in person? Because if so, she could save him the trouble.

"Samantha, there's so much I need to explain to you. About me. About Valerie."

She tensed, not sure she wanted to hear this. She'd been in his apartment a few times, but she couldn't remember seeing any pictures of his fiancée. In fact, the thing that had struck her the most had been his lack of décor.

No pictures of him and his fiancée hung on the walls. No personal knickknacks sat on tables. There was no evidence of a personal previous life. With a frown she wondered if he kept a picture of Valerie in his bedroom. Or had he locked all the visual reminders away deep in his heart?

"You don't need to explain anything to me, Reese. Really, I understand. I know what you're trying to tell me."

"You do?" He looked shocked by her statement.

With a sense of defeat, she nodded. He had come after

her when Dennis had grabbed her. It was only fair she let him off the hook now. "We became close under rather bizarre circumstances, and things moved quickly. Too quickly."

"Marry me."

She blinked. "Excuse me?"

There was a hint of laughter in his eyes. "I thought you knew what I was going to say? Well, this is it. I'm asking if you would please marry me."

Stunned, she stared at him. "But—I thought—You were so..."

Reese dropped beside her on the bench seat, took her hand in his, and slipped a modest diamond ring on her finger. "This ring belonged to my grandmother, but you can choose another if you prefer. Valerie didn't like it and never wore it. I've been thinking about us, about the future. You are so amazing, Samantha, so courageous. I wish I could say the same for me, but I'm slow. It took me a while to admit I've been running from commitment because I was afraid of losing you."

"But I'm not lost," she whispered.

"I know." He smiled, and her heart simply melted. "I'm not lost anymore either. What I had with Valerie was precious, but it also wasn't meant to be. I love you, Samantha. More than I ever thought I'd love anyone again." He cleared his throat. "I know there aren't any guarantees, but I'll take whatever time we're given. Life was meant to be shared with someone you love."

"Oh, Reese." She didn't know what to say.

"So, I'm asking you again, will you please marry me?" His gaze was serious on hers.

She couldn't imagine a more beautiful proposal. For a moment, she gazed down at his grandmother's ring. The setting was dainty with a dazzling center stone. She could hardly believe he cared enough to give her his grandmother's ring. And that Valerie hadn't liked it. Her eyes misted, and she lifted her gaze to his.

"I love you, too, Reese. I learned being with you gives me strength. When you came after me in the Lifeline helicopter, I realized I wanted to fight for a chance at love."

Reese tugged her off the seat and up into his arms. "Build a life with me." He kissed her. "Have children with me." He kissed her again. "Let's live every day to the fullest." He kissed her a third time, lingering over her mouth.

Surrendering her heart to Reese was easy, for he gave her his in return. A true partnership. Everything she'd always wanted.

"Yes." She smiled through her tears. "Starting now and for the rest of our lives."

Dear Reader,

I hope you enjoyed *A Doctor's Secret*, the second book in my Lifeline Air Rescue series. As a critical care nurse, I was fortunate enough to do a ride along with our very own Flight For Life, and while we didn't have any hard landings, I was able to chat with a pilot who didn't hesitate to share his experiences. The airline industry in general is very safe, but crashes do happen. My heart goes out to anyone who experienced such an event in their lives.

Reviews are very important to authors, so if you enjoyed this story, please take a moment to leave a review at the platform from which you purchased the story. I would be very grateful!

I love hearing from my readers! You can find me through my website at www.laurascottbooks.com, on Facebook at Laura Scott Author, and on Twitter @laurascottbooks. Also take a moment to sign up for my newsletter, I offer an exclusive and free novella to my newsletter subscribers.

Lastly, if you're interested in the next book of the series, *A Doctor's Dilemma*, the first chapter is included here.

Until next time,
Laura Scott

15

A DOCTOR'S DILEMMA

Flight nurse Kate Lawrence swallowed a laugh as she entered the hangar at Lifeline Air Rescue. She'd caught a glimpse of a funny sign on the side of a passing truck and wanted to remember the joke for her granddad.

Katie girl, laughter is the best medicine. If people would learn to laugh more, you nurses would be out of a job. He was always trying to top her jokes, having passed along his quirky sense of humor to her. She needed to call him after work anyway, to make sure he was doing all right. Her parents were gone on their three-week European anniversary trip, and she promised to look after him.

She entered the debriefing room to find Lifeline pilot Reese Jarvis and Dr. Ethan Weber, the senior emergency medicine resident, on duty. Both already seated and apparently waiting for her. Was she late? She glanced at the clock to make sure she hadn't lost five minutes someplace. Nope, it was five minutes before seven. Whew. Reese grinned, but Ethan scowled.

"It's about time," Ethan snapped. "We've been waiting."

"Sorry." Even his bad mood wasn't enough to wipe the mirth from her face. The sign flashed in her mind again, making her grin.

"You think that's funny?"

"No, the sign I saw on the plumber's truck was funny. The slogan painted along the side of his van read: *Don't sleep with the drip, call me!*" She giggled. "I wonder how many women actually call him every day? Can you imagine?"

Reese chuckled, but Ethan seemed to have been born without the humor gene because he stared at her for a long moment as if she were some sort of alien species he needed to dissect and name. Finally, he looked away.

"Now that you're here, we can get started." He looked at the off-coming shift doctor, Zane Taylor, and Ivan Ames the paramedic on duty. "How did everything go last night? Any problems?"

The fact that Ethan didn't find the plumber slogan funny almost made her burst into another fit of giggles. Kate bit down hard on her lip to get herself under control. Humor was a good thing; she was a firm believer in the healing power of laughter. Her goal was to laugh every day, but clearly the handsome flight doctor didn't share her view. He wasted no time in getting down to business.

She remembered Ethan from the classroom training, but she hadn't flown with him before today. Since they'd just finished the final sessions a few days ago, it was possible this was one of his first solo flights. If so, maybe that explained why he was so uptight. Then again, he'd been seriously intense during the educational classes, too. And now that she thought about it, she couldn't remember ever seeing him so much as smile.

Hmm. Time to change that attitude.

"We responded to two flight calls during the night,"

Zane reported. "One was an ICU to ICU transfer. A nineteen-year-old male college student diagnosed with Wegner's disease was transported from Cedar Bluff Hospital to Trinity Medical Center with eight chest tubes, and—"

"Eight?" Ethan interrupted. "Not eight. You're kidding, right?"

Zane pursed his lips and slowly shook his head. "Not kidding. I counted. There were eight."

"Why on earth would anyone put in eight chest tubes? I've never heard of such a thing."

"I don't know, but I called the accepting physician to make sure he knew about them." Zane shrugged. "He did, so we took off. Luckily, the transport went off without a hitch."

"We'll need to do a post-flight follow-up visit," Ethan muttered. "Hope the poor kid makes it."

"He will." Kate spoke firmly because, along with humor, she also believed in positive thinking.

"Our second flight was a scene call, car versus tree," Zane continued. "Driver was intoxicated and suffered multiple injuries but should do all right. We transported him to Trinity Medical Center as well."

"Uh-oh. Score one for the tree, driver has a big goose egg," Kate joked with a wince. Medical humor could be a little on the grim side.

Ethan ignored her. "Weather conditions?"

Reese spoke up. "Temperature in the mid-forties Fahrenheit. Winds may be a problem—coming out of the north, gusting up to thirty miles per hour. No precipitation expected, though." Reese flashed a grin. "Hey, what can you expect from your average Wisconsin spring day?"

"Any pending flight calls?" Ethan wanted to know.

"Nope." Zane yawned widely. "You're in waiting mode. Anything else? I'd like to head home. I'm beat."

"Drive carefully." Ethan still didn't smile as he stood and slipped out of the debriefing room, heading for the lounge.

"What is up with him?" she wondered out loud, staring after him with a puzzled frown.

Reese shrugged. "He's new. I don't know much about him. Maybe he's nervous."

"Could be." She was willing to give the somber physician the benefit of the doubt. She didn't remember doing anything during training to merit such a standoffish response. Her gaze swung back to Reese. "Was Sam nervous during her first flight?"

"Yeah." Reese's eyes lit up at the mention of his new wife. The wedding had been small, but very romantic. Kate had shed a few tears when Dr. Samantha Kearn had become Dr. Samantha Jarvis. "She was but claimed my voice helped keep her calm and steady."

"I believe it." Kate had to admit, listening to Reese's husky voice in her headset was no hardship. Then she grinned. "Bet that trick won't work with Ethan."

Reese's eyes widened in horror. "I hope not."

Kate laughed and immediately felt better as she followed Ethan into the lounge. Obviously, she and Ethan had gotten off to a bad start, although she didn't know why. She shrugged. Since Ethan would be around for the next three months and would no doubt spend at least a few shifts as her flying partner, she figured she better make amends.

Her gaze instantly found him, standing next to the leather sofa rummaging in a large backpack. She noticed he was tall and wore his dark hair on the longish side, a dark lock hanging over his forehead as he bent to his task. His shoulders were broad, tapering to a narrow waist, overemphasized perhaps by his one-piece navy blue flight suit. The dark shadow of his beard should have been a turn off, but on him, the disheveled look was very sexy. Her pulse kicked up a notch.

Whoa there, she pulled herself up short. She wasn't the type to fall for a great-looking face. Not that she didn't like men, she did. But over the years her relationships had developed the same, predictable pattern. They started as two people out to share a good time, never managing to progress into anything romantic. The men she went out with seemed to prefer remaining good friends, nothing more.

She really didn't mind. She knew better than anyone that life was precious, and she had made the choice long ago to be positively cheerful, regardless what spitballs life threw at her.

Another lesson learned from her granddad.

"So, what would you like to do while we are in the wait-for-a-call holding pattern?" Kate crossed the room to open the cabinet above the coffeemaker. "Since all the paperwork is up to date, we have a choice of a deck of cards . . ." She held them up for display. "Or Monopoly." She wrinkled her nose. "I'm terrible at Monopoly, and you're probably a pro, so I vote for the deck of cards. I play a mean game of gin rummy."

"I don't play games. I have things to do." Ethan pulled out a thick notebook and laptop computer. Sinking into the comfortable sofa, he set the notebook near his right hand and turned his attention to the computer screen.

Things? She raised a brow. What sorts of things? Was he studying for his boards already? *All work and no play makes Ethan a very dull boy.* She bit her tongue to avoid saying the cliché that immediately sprang to mind. Kate reluctantly set the deck of cards back in the cupboard, then glanced at Ethan. She'd bet her cherry red convertible that his bad attitude wasn't a result of nervousness. Either he'd taken an instant dislike to her or he simply didn't care enough one way or the other to make an effort to be polite. Whatever the reason, it gnawed at her to know Ethan didn't appreciate the true value of fun.

Fortunately for him, she was the right person to show him the error of his ways.

She watched him for a moment, debating the wisdom of poking her nose where it didn't belong. Not that common sense had ever stopped her before. Ethan's brows were pulled together in a deep frown as if what he read on the screen pained him. She sighed. Maybe he had problems. Hey, who didn't? But problems were much easier to face with a light heart than a heavy one. Dr. Ethan Weber would be a hard nut to crack, but she was up for the challenge.

He needed to be rescued from himself before he started having blood pressure problems or migraines—or something worse, like cancer. A guy in his dire, funless state required the full Kate Lawrence humor therapy treatment. Eventually, when he learned how to laugh at himself again, he'd thank her. They would part as friends when he graduated from his residency in June.

There was a little pang at the idea of letting him go but, actually, one of the reasons she tended to avoid dating the transient flight residents was because they always moved on. Oh, she wasn't averse to going out to simply have fun, and it had been a while since she'd found anyone who needed to be rescued as badly as Ethan did. She enjoyed helping people, and wasn't that the reason she become a nurse? And what was there to lose?

Certainly not her heart. Keeping things light was a way to make friends, not romantic boyfriends. And she wasn't looking for anything more. Besides, most guys she dated didn't seem interested in permanent relationships. Especially once she taught them how to relax and have fun. Once they'd moved on, they remained buddies and pals.

In her humble opinion, you could never have enough friends.

Kate idly strolled the length of the lounge, watching Ethan from the corner of her eye as he meticulously scanned the screen, then took careful notes in the notebook. Curious, she edged closer, trying to see what he was doing. It didn't look like work, at least not by her definition. The header at the top of the screen caught her eye. Good grief, was he actually scrolling through some sort of online dating site?

Perpetually cranky, thirty-something-year-old white male, seeking women of similar age for an emotionless relationship. No one looking for a good time need respond.

She giggled at her own joke. Ethan snapped his head around to glare at her. Whoops. Her eyes widened, and she took a guilty step back. Rule number one: don't poke fun at someone unless they have already learned to poke fun at themselves.

"What are you doing? Looking for a place to live?"

Maybe he wasn't on a dating site, maybe he was on one of those online listings that offered all kinds of services including places to live. If she were honest, she could see how finding a new place to live might be considered work by some people. Although, for her, it would be an adventure. She would love a new place to live. Something nice, upscale, yet allowed cats, maybe with a big pool . . .

"No." He scowled and returned his attention to the screen. Kate's fingers itched to snatch it away so she could read what he was doing for herself.

"Maybe I can help," she offered, inching closer. "If you

tell me what you're looking for, I can help you find what you need."

"I don't need help." Ethan didn't even expend the energy to meet her gaze. "Other than for you to be quiet."

Oh, sure. Was he so clueless he couldn't figure out that holding her tongue was her most difficult personal challenge? For being a nearly graduated emergency medical physician, he certainly wasn't very observant.

Good thing, she wasn't interested in anything more than being a friend to help him lighten up or she might have to take his rebuff personally.

At that moment, the phone rang. Praying for a flight call, Kate pounced on it. "Lifeline Air Rescue, may I help you?"

"Can I talk to my daddy?"

The childish voice in her ear caught her off guard. "Your daddy?" She glanced at Ethan, who was already leveraging himself off the sofa, a dark scowl creasing his forehead under the lock of dark hair. He made his way toward her. "Ah, sure, sweetie, he's right here." She handed him the phone.

"Carly? What's wrong, honey?" Ethan dropped his tone and turned away.

Kate automatically took several steps backward, giving him the privacy he clearly desired.

For once, she was struck dumb. She never would have suspected the grim man had a child. A daughter named Carly. She hadn't even known he was married. Her gaze dropped to his left hand holding the receiver, noting the absence of a ring. Which didn't mean a thing, she told herself just as quickly. Lots of men didn't wear their wedding rings.

"Calm down, Carly. Crying isn't going to help. Where's Mrs. Vanderhoff? Put her on the phone." When Ethan put his hand up to massage his forehead, Kate couldn't help but feel a spurt of sympathy. "Mrs. Vanderhoff, what's wrong?" He listened intently for several seconds, then sighed. "Uh-huh. I see. I'm sorry about that. Yes, I understand, but you know very well I can't leave work in the middle of the shift. I'll be home by seven-thirty p.m., we can talk more then. Goodbye."

Kate remained silent for several long seconds after he hung up the phone. She knew she should pretend she hadn't overheard his every word, but that seemed foolish. Obviously, his daughter was in some sort of trouble. Who was Mrs. Vanderhoff? And inquiring minds wanted to know: Where was Mrs. Dr. Weber?

"Ethan, is your daughter all right?" Kate considered the possibility that he was looking through computer sites to find reliable childcare. Poor thing. Her heart softened. "Maybe I can help."

"She's fine." His tone was clipped. "And I already told you, I don't need your help."

"But—"

"Listen." He spun toward her, his dark eyes flashing with anger. "Stop trying so hard. Can't you see I'm not interested?"

Kate's jaw dropped. "I–wait a minute. I'm just trying to be nice. Don't you recognize friendship when you see it?" She struggled to remain calm, taking a slow deep breath. She knew he'd be difficult, so why the sudden urge to defend herself? His lashing out at her was more than likely related to his distress over his daughter. No reason to take it personally.

Ethan raised a brow. "Friendship? I don't need a friend. If you're not interested in me as a potential date, then you must be nosy. Do me a favor and leave me alone."

Kate ignored the pang of hurt and lifted her hands in mock surrender. Time to back off. "Okay, fine. Forget I asked."

Their pagers beeped in simultaneous chirps. Kate read the message out loud. "Two adult victims of a motorcycle crash." She barely glanced at Ethan as she swung toward the door. "Where's Reese?"

"Last I saw, he was in the debriefing room." Ethan beat her to the doorway, poking his head through the opening and calling out to the pilot. "Reese? Let's go."

The three of them headed out to the hangar where the Lifeline helicopter stood, ready and waiting. Reese jumped into the pilot's seat, gesturing for Kate and Ethan to board as he started the engines. Kate donned her helmet, then grabbed the clipboard and began initiating notes of the response. All this technology and they still hadn't figured out a way to get the flight notes computerized.

She tried to ignore Ethan as he sat beside her in the small confines of the helicopter, but her gaze was continuously drawn to him. *I'm not interested. I don't need a friend. Do me a favor and leave me alone.* His blunt comments shouldn't have lingered like an aching tooth, but they did.

He was different than most men she'd befriended in the past. She was more aware of him on a physical level, her nerve endings tingling just by sitting so close. Very strange. She'd need to work hard to ignore the sensation.

If they hadn't been in a helicopter, heading to the scene of the crash, she might've taken the opportunity to tell him how laughter had been proven to produce more immunoglobulin A and B in the body's bloodstream, these higher levels helping to prevent disease. To explain how humor had been used successfully by physicians in treating high blood pressure in a group of patients where half of them could stop taking their medication completely while the other half used much lower doses. There was even literature proving how using humor in cancer patients dropped their need for pain medication by half.

Reaffirming the facts surrounding the purpose of her mission helped her to relax. Ethan needed her, whether he realized it yet or not. Laughter was a savior, a simple way of turning your whole life around, even when things were bleak. Wasn't she living proof? She'd been through a terrible time, yet she had come out on the other side.

Ethan needed this, not just for himself, but for his daughter. She couldn't help remembering how the hard planes in Ethan's normally stern expression had softened when he'd spoken to his little girl.

Kate firmed her resolve. Carly, like any other child in the world, needed smiles and laughter and fun, too.

Made in the USA
Columbia, SC
27 May 2024